A Very Special Hayseed Christmas

HAYSEED PRESS LLC

Published by Hayseed Press LLC
Cedar Falls, IA
hayseedpress.com

ISBN 979-8-9928776-3-2

Book Cover by Jackson Moore of CHARM Co-op
https://charm.coop/

First edition 2025

CONTENTS

Introduction — 4

1. A Bowtie Affair — 6
   By Jenny Fee

2. The Legend of the Carroll County Christmas Changeling — 23
   By Aaron Narigon

3. The Gnome — 28
   By Cole Thorna

4. The Best Worst Christmas Ever — 44
   By Melinda Wichmann

5. A Taste of Home — 62
   By Roxy Strike

6. Twas A Relatively Minor Night Before Christmas — 82
   By Vicki Minor

7. An Ordinary Winter Day — 88
   By Michael Kaufman

8. Pears in the Pine Tree — 99
   By Katrina Sogaard Anderson

9. White Elephants 112
    By Anne Houghton

10. Anywhere But Iowa 122
    By Marc Dickinson

11. The 2035 Christmas Pie Contest 136
    By Nick Narigon

12. The Failure's Christmas Gift 167
    By Peter Boylan

13. The Christmas Quilt 188
    By Rachel Coltvet Kristenson

14. The Night the Animals Speak 217
    By Dace Carlisle

Other titles from Hayseed Press

Iowa Weird Vol. 1

A short story collection
about the monsters
creeping in the cornfields

A Boy on the Farm

A memoir of growing up on
an Iowa family farm during
the Great Depression

Find these books and more at
hayseedpress.com

INTRODUCTION

Growing up in Cedar Falls, Iowa in the 1980s and '90s, the holiday season was a family affair. On Christmas Eve we had chili and oyster stew (which only my dad ate) and then went to the midnight service at church. Early on Christmas morning, with strict directions not to wake up Mom and Dad until 7 a.m., we opened stockings that were stuffed with oranges, cereal boxes, and school supplies.

Then the real event occurred—the opening of the Christmas presents. Afterwards, we crammed into the minivan to make the rounds to the grandparents' homes in Fort Dodge and Indianola. There was always turkey, mashed potatoes, green bean casserole, yams, and the requisite pies and Christmas cookies.

Along the way, the Christmas album, *A Very Special Christmas*, featuring the likes of Bruce Springsteen, Madonna, Whitney Houston, Annie Lennox, and Run D.M.C., provided the soundtrack—and continues to this day.

At our house today we start playing Christmas music on November 1. However, our family traditions veer off course from there. My wife is Japanese, and our sons were born in Tokyo. It always tickled me when a skinny Japanese Santa showed up at their daycare to hand out presents.

The family holiday in Japan is New Year's Eve. On New Year's Day we gather at my wife's childhood home where her mother presents foods in the traditional *osechi ryori* spread.

The customary foods like black soybeans, herring roe, rolled omelets, and shrimp, some of which take weeks to prepare, are beautifully arranged in a three-tiered box covered in red or black lacquer and gold leaf. Then you sit around the table all day feasting and drinking sake.

When we moved to Singapore the boys' international school recognized Christmas along with Diwali, Ramadan, and Chinese New Year. Now that we live in New York, Rosh Hashanah and Yom Kippur are recognized as school holidays.

While *A Very Special Hayseed Christmas* focuses on the Christmas traditions of Iowa, our writers come from different backgrounds and each of their stories reflect their multi-cultural backgrounds.

Some of the stories we share here reflect customs from the European homeland, and there are similar themes throughout. While two of our writers have Filipino heritage, and their stories give insight to their unique family traditions.

Some of the stories delve into the darker side of Christmas, while we have a couple of whimsical holiday poems. And then there are stories that add a little spice to the holiday cheer.

Whether you are traveling this holiday season or plan to curl up by the fireplace, *A Very Special Hayseed Christmas* is the perfect companion to keep you warm and entertained.

Merry Christmas and Happy Holidays!

—Nick Narigon
Co-founder Hayseed Press
hayseed@hayseedpress.com

1

A BOWTIE AFFAIR

BY JENNY FEE

Melvin MacFee was not in the holiday spirit.

There was not a solitary strand of tinsel in his room at Shady Grove Assisted Living. Not a single wrapped gift or tin foil-covered plate of confections.

In fact, when he heard a couple of nurse's aides outside his door snickering about him being a real "Scrooge MacFee," his 82-year-old heart panged for only an instant.

Fine by me, he thought, shooing away any embarrassment. *Never liked Christmas anyway.*

Oh, but that wasn't true at all. There was a time when Melvin still lived on the farm with Edith, their daughter's family just down the road. He'd never had much time for them during planting or harvest but come December he always saw to it that his granddaughter's sled was in prime working condition, that his Santa suit in the back of the closet still fit.

But those days were long gone, buried with Edith and all the bickering that followed.

What had Melvin and his daughter fought about anyway? Sometimes at night, when Melvin couldn't sleep, he would wheel himself to his window and look out at the hay field next to Shady Grove, trying to remember.

This, the first of December, was one of those nights. Yet the dormant field held no answers in the moonlight, just as it hadn't when the alfalfa bloomed or lay in long windrows.

Melvin felt the corners of his eyes moisten. *Must only work from on top a tractor*, he thought, *or when it's your own field*. He used to look out onto his land from his John Deere and always find the memories or epiphanies he sought.

He backed away from the window, careful not to bump into the dresser for fear of toppling his collection of photo frames. Heaven knows he'd already done that a time or two. The oval wedding portrait now had a jagged crack right down the middle.

He hardly noticed, though. Edith had been such a beauty in her tea-length gown, her red hair swept into a bouffant. Melvin had cleaned up pretty good himself with a fresh crewcut, white suit jacket and black bow tie—a special request from Edith. But he knew she was out of his league.

Still, she had a way of making him forget he was just a poor farmer and she could've had her pick of suitors. *Dean Martin's got nothing on you!* she'd told him after their wedding, in a quiet moment alone when she'd straightened his bow tie and leaned in for a kiss not suitable for the altar.

No, he hadn't always been a Scrooge. He'd been callused hands and scruffy beard and worn overalls, but he'd loved Edith just like one of those heroes in a Hollywood movie.

And he'd loved their little girl and, in time, her little girl. Melvin studied their photos, too, each a Shirley Temple lookalike in her youth.

He could hear Cindy chattering at him while he worked to repair the combine, Joslyn's gleeful scream as she zipped down her favorite sledding hill.

"Grandpa, you built me the fastest sled in the world!" Joslyn said to him once, flinging herself into his arms at the bottom of the hill. Her pint-sized body hit with such force that they both toppled into a snow drift.

Edith had managed to capture the next moment with her Polaroid: Melvin back on his feet with so much snow in his beard that he looked like St. Nick himself, Joslyn hugging his leg and looking up at him with wild eyes and sheer adoration.

Was that really just a few years ago? Melvin stopped his wheelchair in front of his television and absentmindedly flipped through the channels, knowing he was in for yet another sleepless night.

If not for those photos, he thought, it could've all been just an old man's dream.

***

"Please, Mr. MacFee? Just for a few minutes? It's not good for body or soul to live like a hermit."

Melvin tried his best to glare at Wanda, but she was his favorite aide—the only one who actually talked with him and didn't look at him like he was a piece of dusty furniture.

Still, he could summon a little growl for what she was asking of him.

"Nope. Won't do it," he replied, intentionally making a to-do of setting the brakes on his wheelchair and folding his arms across his chest. "I don't like Christmas, and I don't like kids. Too much commotion."

It was the same posture he'd assumed when asked about Sleigh Bell Bingo, Christmas Carol Karaoke, a rousing afternoon of mini-marshmallow art, and an ambitious but perpetually sharp performance of Handel's *Messiah* by the local high school choir.

Melvin had yet to regret missing anything. No, it was peaceful in his room where one of Edith's patchwork quilts decorated his bed and the clothes in his closet still held a whiff of the hog house.

His old '70s-green recliner had the stuffing poking out in places, but it'd been his roost to watch the evening news alongside Edith every night. If he looked closely, he could even spot a few white hairs from Snowball, the cat that Melvin had always referred to as That Mangy Old Thing but had secretly adored.

"Is that a smile?" Wanda asked, jolting him to the present. "Please, Mr. MacFee. These are eighth graders. Calm ones. And they've brought Christmas goodies. It'd be nice to at least make an appearance."

Melvin looked over the flannel pajamas he was still wearing at two in the afternoon. Knew his beard was straggly—not at all like when Edith would help him trim it. No, it was only "making an appearance" if your absence would be felt, not save embarrassment.

"Oh, Melvin," Wanda sighed, doing away with decorum in her frustration. "It's like you're determined to be miserable here. Don't you know I can't stand that?"

As soon as she left the room, Melvin felt a pang of guilt. When did he become a grumpy old man? Wanda was his friend, and it wasn't every day that school kids came to visit. Maybe he'd rightfully earned the title of "Scrooge MacFee" after all.

He decided it'd be best to sleep the afternoon away. He wheeled back to the window, settling in to watch the snow fall and welcoming the quick heaviness of his eyelids.

It was pretty, really, like a life-sized snow globe that he wished he could step into. Wouldn't it be something to play in the snow again…

Just as Melvin drifted off, his door burst open. First, a girl barreled in, screeching to a halt in the middle of his room. Then Wanda tiptoed in, staying closer to the door as though bracing for a fresh round of his grumbling.

"Well, maybe not so calm," she mumbled, eyeing the youngster who somehow seemed to fill the entire space despite her willowy frame. Her eyes gleamed like a little wild thing, and there was a bold blue streak in her otherwise golden hair.

She eyed Melvin with an intensity well beyond her years. She didn't seem to think he was Scrooge, he mused, as the haze of sleep left him. Maybe Jacob Marley's ghost?

Not quite. When she finally broke the silence, it was with a single, shocking word:

"Grandpa?"

***

Dear Diary,

You won't believe what happened during our field trip today.

The guy I was matched with wouldn't come out to the dining room like all the other old people. That was fine by me, but this nurse must've thought I looked sad or something because she told me to follow her.

Um, OK. I didn't really want to, but now I'm glad that I did. It wasn't just some old dude. It was Grandpa!!!

He didn't believe it at first, but I pointed to my picture in his room and reminded him about how we used to go sledding. Then he cried and his nurse cried. Super awkward.

But now what am I going to do? If Mom finds out, there's no way she'll let me go back again with my class. But I don't think she was really even listening when I told her about going in the first place, so maybe she won't ask about how it went?

I've missed Grandpa. I don't know what happened to make Mom so mad at him. So, I'm keeping this a secret until I can figure out how to get him back for good.

***

Melvin may have avoided marshmallow art, but the following week he found himself gluing cotton ball after cotton ball to a paper plate.

Ridiculous, he thought, but not so bad with Joslyn sitting next to him. They'd quickly settled into a routine of her squeezing glue for the next placement and him fumbling to put the cotton in its spot—with added bravado to make her giggle.

"Does it look like a snowman yet?" he joked at their messy creation, winking at his granddaughter. "We could show these folks a thing or two about making a real snowman."

The girl's eyes lit up. "Or sledding! That was the best."

It was bittersweet for Melvin, thinking of all the talks and outings they'd missed the past five years. Yet here he was with Joslyn now, enjoying a silly craft project with a side of lukewarm hot cocoa and holiday tunes drifting from the radio at the nurse's station.

A Christmas miracle if there ever was one. Other resident-schoolkid pairs were spread out across the sprawling dining room, unaware of Melvin and Joslyn's reunion.

He studied the blue streak in her locks. A few days ago, he might've rolled his eyes at such a thing on another child, but it was becoming on Joslyn.

"I must've kept you out in the cold too much all those years ago," Melvin mused, nearly touching her hair with his clumsy hand but stopping himself. Too many years had passed. "You've got a frozen spot here!"

Joslyn looked at him perplexed for a second, then snorted. "Ha! Oh, you're funny. I keep that streak in my hair for Autism Awareness in honor of Sam."

Now Melvin was the confused one. Sam? The name was familiar yet faraway all at once, like so many memories these days.

He knew better than to ask for a reminder. Even from Wanda, that usually got him a look of stunned surprise, then sadness. The last thing he wanted was to see those expressions on his account on his beautiful granddaughter's face.

She did look troubled, though, as she squeezed the last dot of glue on the paper plate.

"Grandpa, are you sad here? You had a whole farm, and now you just have a little room. And," she added, lowering her voice, "it doesn't smell good here."

Melvin felt equal parts ready to laugh and cry. "Well, it's not so bad," he replied, after giving careful consideration his answer. "Don't you remember that the hogs didn't smell too good either?

"And there's a pretty little field right outside my window," he went on. "When I look at it, especially at night, I can almost make believe it's my old field and I'm back on my John Deere. I can just picture you and your mom and your grandma walking out to see me for a coffee break."

Joslyn had been keeping her eyes glued to the paper plate, but she turned them squarely toward Melvin now. They were the same as Cindy's, he realized, the palest shade of blue and capable of seeing right through him.

"That's good, Grandpa. But I have to ask—I need to know—what happened?" she asked. "Why'd we stop visiting you after Grandma died?"

Melvin felt memories start to swirl up in his mind, like ghosts stirring in the corners of a graveyard. His first instinct was to bat them away, but he strained to see them instead. Such terrible meanness—on his part and Cindy's—while Edith lay in a hospital bed.

"Jolly," Melvin began, calling Joslyn by her long-ago nickname without thinking about it, "do you remember what I told you about hurt animals?"

After briefly scanning her own memories, she nodded her head emphatically. "Yes. That I should come and get you if I ever found one," she answered. "That even the nicest animal might claw or bite at me if it's scared or hurt enough."

"That's right," Melvin said, proud that she'd remembered and relieved that his explanation just might work. "Well, people aren't so different. When your grandma was sick, your mom and I were hurting something terrible. Instead of helping each other, we started clawing at each other—saying things we never should've. And I suppose we're both too stubborn to say we're sorry."

"Are you?" Joslyn asked, her eyes locked on his.

"Every single day. And if I ever get a chance, I'll tell her so."

Joslyn smiled and resumed gluing, only to have her eyebrows bunch together again.

"So, what are we going to do? Next week is the last time my class comes here... for the big party," she said, hushing to a near-whisper as though nervous her classmates might catch on. "I won't get to see you again after that. Not unless I can talk Mom into visiting. And, well..."

Melvin had to strain to hear her voice, so much so that he only heard half of her words. Even still, he understood. It'd been worrying him, too—just how short lived their reunion could be.

"We can invite our parents to the party," Joslyn continued, anxiety making her louder. "But should I? Maybe she'd see you and have a change of heart. Or maybe it would be a major catastrophe."

Melvin couldn't help but smile at "catastrophe," despite the real threat of one. Was that Edith coming out in her? Was Joslyn a reader like her grandma, a collector of the words she found in books? It occurred to Melvin that it was yet another thing about his granddaughter that he didn't know anymore.

"Well," he said, trying to focus better on the matter at hand, "that is a very good question. I'm not sure your mom even knows I'm here... or thinks of it anyway. I was at a different place when I first moved off the farm. What do you think she'd think of seeing me again? It'd be an awful big surprise."

"It would be," Joslyn agreed, sighing as she stood to shrug on her winter coat. Her classmates were all doing the same at their teacher's bidding. "And maybe that'd help us. She might get all sappy to see you before she can remember how much she hates you. Bye!"

With that, she was sprinting across the room. Melvin started to reach for her out of habit, expecting a bear hug like when she was little, but quickly let his arms drop to his sides.

He felt deflated for a bigger reason, though. *Hate?*

He'd convinced himself over the years that his daughter was too busy to see him. No, they hadn't parted on the best of terms, but she'd always been closer to Edith. Had a successful career and the kids to watch after. Melvin figured he was neglected, not despised.

Kids. As Joslyn gave him a quick wave before filing out with her classmates, the realization hit Melvin: He had a grandson. Sam. The boy had been in diapers when they'd seen each other last.

Melvin drained his cup of cocoa, hoping that no one—especially Wanda—noticed his tears.

***

No one was going to compare Melvin to Dean Martin these days, but even he had to admit he didn't look too shabby.

He wheeled closer to the mirror on the front of his closet door for closer inspection. With Wanda's help, he'd swapped out his usual flannel pajamas for a button-down plaid shirt, olive-green sweater that Edith had knitted for him, and a never-worn pair of sweatpants.

Wanda had even trimmed up his beard for him, whittled down his bushy eyebrows, and smoothed his hair with a little pomade that she'd brought from home.

"Well, look at who was hiding under there!" she'd exclaimed afterward, causing the color in Melvin's already-rosy cheeks to deepen. "You're going to turn heads today for sure."

You've got that right, Melvin thought, butterflies beginning to swirl in his belly. Today was the big Christmas party that was the grand finale of Shady Grove's adopt-a-grandparent program. Joslyn might be back with an unsuspecting Cindy in tow.

Dare he hope for a tearful reunion? Or would Cindy do a double take, then march out of the nursing home? Melvin wasn't sure his heart could take the latter. Maybe it would have been better to part ways with Joslyn last week, just thankful for their couple of visits together…

A knock at the door jolted Melvin, but it was Wanda's smiling face that peeked around.

"You ready?" she asked, looking at him with a fondness and anticipation more fitting for a graduation or wedding day than a humble Christmas party. "They should be here any minute. Remember… just be your charming self."

Was he charming? Edith had thought so. Both Cindy and Joslyn when they were younger, too. Melvin struggled to remember what had made him so likeable back then.

That's when it occurred to him: he needed a finishing touch!

Too distracted to answer Wanda, he wheeled to the antique cigar box on his dresser. He knew its contents by heart: the first note that Edith had ever written to him back in home economics class, a toy soldier he'd carried everywhere as a kid, a stack of Cindy and Joslyn's school pictures, and his bow tie.

Hadn't that always transformed Melvin into somebody special? He'd worn it for his wedding, of course, but also the girls' baptisms and graduations.

He spun around and held it out to Wanda, a wordless request for help.

"Well, now you've done it," she murmured, winking at him as she stepped forward to comply. "If your daughter doesn't come around today, I'm officially adopting you."

And that was a big if, Melvin thought, as he wheeled behind Wanda into the dining room, his bow tie fitted snugly around his neck. But despite his fretting, he was stunned by the room's transformation courtesy of the nursing staff.

Strands of Christmas lights surrounded every window and swirled around every Greek-style column. Each square tabletop was "wrapped" as though a massive gift, complete with a billowy bow in the middle as a centerpiece and a "tag" bearing the names of the resident-student pair meant to sit there.

The aroma of spiced apple cider wafted from a slow cooker plugged in at the nurses' station, where "Rockin' Around the Christmas Tree" also belted from a radio. And the staff—Wanda included—had all suddenly donned a pair of reindeer antlers or elf's hat.

"Care for a refreshment?" she asked Melvin, jerking her head dramatically toward a table of cookies so that her hat's jingle bell would ring. "Gingerbread, sugar, or your favorite, divinity."

Melvin eyed the white, melt-in-your mouth candies that had been Edith's specialty. So that's why Wanda had asked whether he had the recipe—which he did, of course, in Edith's old recipe box. It was a comfort to him to flip through the notecards, nearly all in her delicate handwriting.

"Thank you," he said, his voice thick with emotion. He already knew they couldn't be as good as Edith's, but it would surely be a taste of all those Christmases back on the farm.

Melvin felt nearly as light and airy as divinity candy himself. Perhaps this wasn't going to be a catastrophe, as Joslyn had feared.

Why, the dining room had been transformed into a winter wonderland. And just look at all the staff—and Melvin himself!—made over with holiday flair. This was going to be a good day indeed.

Melvin found his spot at one of the tables, took a gentlemanly nibble of his piece of divinity, and straightened his tie. His family would find him the picture of confidence and contentment.

And that's when the door of the nursing home burst open and a crowd of schoolkids and their parents rushed in. Melvin squinted to look for Joslyn, but his memory still had him looking for a third grader with pigtails and missing front teeth.

By the time he spotted her, she *and* Cindy had already noticed him. He couldn't hear what his daughter was saying to his granddaughter, but she looked angry. Gestured wildly with her hands the way she always did when emotions ran high.

"No!" he could hear Joslyn wail. She looked at him just then with such sorrow that Melvin was sure that he felt his heart crack right down the middle, just like the broken glass of the wedding picture back in his room.

He scrambled for the brakes of his wheelchair, desperate to cross the room to them before they could leave. When had the dining room become so large? His arthritic hands, suddenly shaking, could only fumble with the chair's latches.

"I'm sorry!" he began to shout, looking at his daughter. "Cindy-Girl, wait! Daddy's sorry!"

Had she heard him? After what seemed like the slightest pause, she grabbed Joslyn's hand, and they were out the door. Gone.

Melvin looked wildly around the room, panic rising in his chest. What could he do now? Where was Wanda?

The bow tie that he'd been wearing so proudly moments before now seemed to choke him. The crumbs of divinity in the back of his mouth made him gag.

Melvin MacFee's only transformation today was that of a lonely old man into a pathetic old fool.

***

Dear Diary,

Today was a major catastrophe. I mean, the WORST. Mom wouldn't even go over to see Grandpa. Wouldn't even let me say goodbye.

How is that the Christmas spirit? Adults are such hypocrites. Peace, goodwill—blah, blah, blah.

It felt like a Christmas MIRACLE that I got paired with my actual grandpa for adopt-a-grandparent. Doesn't Mom get it?

And then she cried the whole way driving home. Well, I don't get that! If I supposedly hated somebody, I wouldn't shed a single tear for them.

Adults make everything way too complicated. I'm going to tell her if she ever comes out of her bathroom. She ruined our second chance for all of us to be a family again. What would Grandma Edith say about that?!

***

Melvin didn't touch his supper, just as he hadn't all week. It didn't matter that it was Christmas Eve dinner. He felt at least a tiny bit of gratification as he watched the gravy coagulate atop the instant mashed potatoes.

Wanda came back for his tray just as Melvin flipped off his TV for the night. No need to watch "It's a Wonderful Life." He knew it wasn't.

"Mr. MacFee, please," Wanda begged. "I know you don't want to be here for Christmas. Shoot, I'd rather not be here working a double shift either. But can't we try to make the most of it? You tell me what sounds good for Christmas dinner, and I'll go see if can rustle it up."

Melvin didn't look at Wanda, just kept staring at the dark TV screen.

"Not hungry," he grumbled. But, swearing he could feel Wanda wince, he added, "Thank you, Wanda. You're a good nurse and a good friend."

When he heard her grab his tray and shut the door behind her, he rolled to his window. He held his hand to it, feeling cold radiate from the other side of the glass. A fresh blanket of snow spread across the farm field that he liked to imagine was his own. The sky was clear, the moon especially bright as it often seemed to be on the coldest winter nights.

A doe and two half-grown fawns ambled across the expanse of white. They meandered a few feet, then stopped as though getting their bearings. Crept forward again. Could they hear coyotes in the distance? A car rumbling to life in the parking lot behind the building?

Melvin's eyelids grew heavy. His empty stomach rumbled. The old alarm clock tick-tick-ticked on the nightstand behind him, next to his bed.

In time, the ticking grew louder. Not the hands of a clock, Melvin realized, but a fist lightly knocking on his window.

Joslyn.

Was he dreaming? The girl grinned, her face rimmed by the faux-fur edging of her hood. She waved at him with her mitten-covered hand, then gestured behind her.

Not a doe and two fawns. Cindy and Joslyn and Sam—the first grader waddling gleefully in a puffy snowsuit. By the light of the moon and stars, Melvin could see they were all smiling at him now.

His door opened and Wanda stepped back inside, gently taking his hand to place a note in the center of his palm.

"Looks like you're not stuck with me, after all, Melvin," she said. "I'll be by in the morning to help you get ready."

He didn't wait for Wanda to leave again before opening the note. He didn't know what Joslyn's handwriting looked like anymore, he realized, but there was no doubt it was hers.

Dear Grandpa,

Mom says she's sorry, too. She says you two had too many good years to let some sad times ruin everything. We've all missed you. We'll pick you up at 10 tomorrow morning for breakfast and to open presents.

P.S. It was my idea to surprise you in "your" field tonight! Just like the old days when it was time for a coffee break. Sneaky, huh? Best Christmas EVER!!!

Melvin didn't take his eyes off his family, who were all waving now as they began plodding back to their car. But he quickly called over his shoulder to Wanda before she could leave his room again.

"Wanda, did you hear? *I'll be home for Christmas,*" Melvin said, breaking into song with his best Bing Crosby impression. "Wanda—my Christmas angel—where's my bow tie?"

***

About the Author

Jenny Fee works as an award-winning journalist, seventh-generation Iowa farmer, and volunteer publicist for a bustling cat rescue. She lives with her husband on a historic 1855 farm that they restored from near ruin with the help of family. When a fresh blanket of snow covers its three red barns and dozens of evergreen trees, it could double as a holiday postcard—unless one of her pet goats or show pigs is on the loose.

2

THE LEGEND OF THE CARROLL COUNTY CHRISTMAS CHANGELING

By Aaron Narigon

I t is said that in the year 1899, in the manger of a freezing hausbarn somewhere near Carroll, Iowa, a baby was born early in the wee hours of December 6th. Alone because of the deep snow, the birth had been a long and difficult one, and the new parents succumbed to exhaustion and fell into a deep slumber.

With the light of day came the understanding that the child was unusual. One might even argue, ugly. A lot of newborns looked odd right after birth, and that was what they told themselves those first days. But the boy kept a bluish tint, like he didn't get enough air, and his sparse hair was shock white. His head seemed too large for his body, his mouth too large for his head. His eyes couldn't seem to stay in one place long, and he drooled everywhere.

Though sickly looking, it ate as often as it could, with only small breaks before it would cry again for more and more and more. The young mother did the best she could, but soon she could not keep up and by the next day they were giving it cow milk, then goat milk as well.

On the third day the babe was crawling, and they found it suckling straight from the cow. When the baby wasn't feeding or throwing a tantrum it was destroying things. Tools, utensils, clothes, the mother's handiwork, whenever left alone for an instant it found something important and ransacked it. The husband became upset, but his wife told him to have patience. So, he fixed what broke as best he could.

On the fourth day, the husband's grandmother arrived. She was ancient and tough as a bur oak and her ways were of the Old World. After she had heard the news of the newborn over the party line, she had traveled through waist deep snow for a day and a night and a day without stopping.

When she first saw the baby she gasped and made a sign in the air. She asked with urgency if they had hung iron in the crib, swaddled it in the father's clothes, or at the least kept constant vigilance over the crib until the babe could be baptized? They confessed they had done none of that, and so the grandmother was certain. This was a changeling in their crib. An elf woman or troll woman or hill woman had swapped in her malformed child that first night and stolen their baby!

The wife and husband didn't believe her. The wife was ever loving and a place of solace for the troubled, famished little being.

On the fifth day the baby began to eat grain. He followed the horses and cattle as they stomped it out and he ate it right from the ground.

On the sixth day the grandmother tried to beat the baby with a wooden spoon. When she finally got him cornered, they stopped her. She insisted the hill woman would come to save the baby if only they would let her beat it. They did not.

On the seventh day the baby began to eat the eggs whole, and they had to fish the shells out of his mouth.

On the ninth day the grandmother tried to stab it with iron knitting needles. When they took the needles away, she protested that the ladies on the party line agreed this was the best way to reveal the babe's true parents.

On the tenth day the baby began to eat salted meat and raw onions and the sauerkraut.

On the twelfth day after bedtime the grandmother tried to stake the baby to the midden heap. What elf woman lets her baby smell and suffer so, she asked as they untied it?

On the fourteenth day the boy began to toddle around.

On the fifteenth day the grandmother tried to drown it in the water trough. No troll woman lets her baby touch water, she asserted as they dried it off.

On the sixteenth day the baby began saying, "momma."

On the eighteenth day the grandmother tried to throw it in the baking oven. The story goes that the mother broke down into tears then. Some say she had cried herself to sleep every night since the birth, but all agree at this time she surrendered to her tears.

The husband made the grandmother sleep in the old sod house out back that night. He didn't know what to do. Their larder, store of grain, and root cellar had almost been cleared, and it was not yet Christmas.

The next night, on Christmas Eve, the family came together again. They burned a yule log, sang Christmas songs, ate the last of their salted meat and candies, and lit candles on the Christmas tree. Then the grandmother asked them to pray with her. They bowed their heads, and she asked the spirits of Christmas to visit and bless the family, and to forgive her.

When they looked up, everyone says, they had guests. Father Christmas, Belsnickel, and the Christmas Woman were out that night and answered the prayer.

The Christmas Woman came forward. She admitted the changeling was her child, born out of wedlock so she hid the elfling. It took so much for her to recover from childbirth, care for and hide her special child, and serve Belsnickel in their holiday duties.

The extra burdens of Nikolaustag broke her and at this rural house, while the parents slept and Belsnickel looked for the newborn's shoe, she had made the switch. She was overwhelmed with guilt and had missed the little elfling ever since.

Everyone agrees she then removed from a harness in the folds of her dress the human baby and gave him to his shocked mother and father. Then she took up the elfling and held him close. Some people say later that Father Christmas chastised Belsnickel for making the elf women work so soon after giving birth, and others whispered that Belsnickel was even the father of the Christmas Woman's son and had known about the whole affair.

The Christmas Spirits left them with blessings and gifts of clothes, food, grain, and sweets. And the family cherished the returned boy, who looked healthy and had been well-cared for. The mother then insisted upon the Christmas Woman that every busy holiday season she must bring the elfling to them and the family would watch and keep the elfling safe until her rounds were over and the new year had begun.

On the twentieth day it was Christmas Day, and it warmed enough the snow melted down and friends, neighbors, and family arrived to celebrate. The mother and father shared with everyone the gifts of food and clothes from the Christmas Spirits, and they were given many more in return.

And the story goes that the human boy grew up fairer, stronger, taller, and wiser than his brothers, his sisters, his parents, and his peers, having nursed from a faerie spirit to start his life. He enlisted as a young man, went away to serve in the Great War and did great things and helped many people, and lived an extremely long and blessed life.

And before he left, each and every holiday season his family entertained a special guest, who they loved and cherished forever as one of their own.

***

About the Author

Hayseed Press co-founder Aaron Narigon holds a Master of Arts in English Language and Literature from University of Northern Iowa. He is a Professor of English and has taught at Hawkeye Community College since 2002. Currently Aaron coordinates Middlemoot, the Midwest's premier biennial Tolkien conference, and is the co-editor of UKL, the only scholarly journal dedicated to the work of Ursula K. LeGuin.

3
THE GNOME

By Cole Thorna

Ruckus, Iowa is home to a gnome. On December 1st of every year, a citizen of the town places a garden gnome some place conspicuous. The gnome stands a foot-and-a-half high. It beams a toothy grin surrounded by a white terracotta beard. It has bright blue, painted-on eyes and a pale red cap. It gestures towards the sky with an open palm as if to say *check this out. Isn't this great?*

The gnome is two hundred years old, and once sat in the garden of Phillip Ruckus, the founder of the town. There's a daguerreotype photograph of Phillip and his family standing in front of their luscious and bountiful garden. Next to the youngest girl in the picture is the gnome, smiling resolutely and gesturing to the sepia sky: *check this out. Isn't this great?* The photograph looms large in Ruckus' City Hall. Underneath there is a placard that reads:

Ruckus, Iowa. The City of the Gnome.

***

A Ruckus city garbage truck thumps and rattles down Main Street. Dawn has yet to break; the empty strip of shops and restaurants is lit by the headlights of the mammoth vehicle. An occasional snowflake falls onto the windshield then disappears.

Travis rests his head against the window. He sits in the passenger seat of the garbage truck listening to his companion complain.

"And after going to that money pit for three semesters, she just wants to switch up? Marine biology? How does marine biology have anything to do with English?" says Harry. He presses on the brake, and the garbage truck squeals to a slow halt.

"You wanna take turns?" Harry asks, indicating the black metal trash receptacle they've stopped alongside.

"Why would we take turns?" Travis asks.

Harry shrugs. "It's cold."

Travis rolls his eyes as he opens the passenger door. His boots land on the pavement and he walks over to the trash receptacle that is bolted into the sidewalk. He lifts out the inner plastic can, walks to the back of the truck, and throws the contents inside. He returns the plastic can to the trash receptacle. Harry gives him a big smile and a thumbs up.

Travis walks down the block, towards the next trash can so that he can repeat the process. The truck follows his slow trot down the street.

Travis freezes in place.

Hidden from view of the street, placed with its back resting against the metal of the receptacle, is the famous Ruckus gnome. Travis stares at it. He stares into its bright blue eyes, regards its large toothy smile. The gnome stares back. It gestures to the lightening sky.

Check this out. Isn't this great?

Without a sound or as much as a blink, Travis winds his foot back and swings it forward with all the force his slim frame can muster. His boot contacts the gnome's brittle face. He feels the back of its clay head slam into the metal. He feels his toe go all the way through the gnome to the other side. The trash receptacle makes a *DING* sound that echoes up and down Main Street. Pain flares up Travis' leg, and he stumbles back.

There are chunks of gnome face strewn around the sidewalk. Bits of his beard. Its pale red hat. Its plump, two-hundred-year-old nose. One completely intact blue eye stares up at Travis.

Travis stares at the mess he's made. Stares at the headless torso of the gnome still propped up against the side of the receptacle. He tries to count the number of chunks he's made. He gets to thirteen before he's interrupted.

When Harry sees the gnome, and the state that it's in, he doubles over, hands on his knees, wide eyes unable to remove themselves from the destruction before him.

"Is that..." Harry starts, still in a state of denial. Travis doesn't answer him. Harry wheezes as he takes in the carnage. "It's December first," he says, remembering.

Travis glances at the distressed man. His eyes are caught in a streetlight. They're dancing around as tears are on the verge of streaming down Harry's face.

"Uh," says Travis sheepishly. "Yeah. I forgot it was December first already. That thing came out of nowhere, scared the hell out of me."

Slowly, Harry turns his head to look Travis in the face. "I saw you. You stopped, looked down, *then* kicked."

Travis is silent.

"What the hell did you *do?*"

"It's just a gnome!" Travis blurts out. His words sound hollow, as if even he knows they're untrue.

"Just a… just a gnome…" Harry forces a laugh and paces the sidewalk. He points towards Travis. "You're clinical kid. You are absolutely clinical."

In the distance, the two men hear a car door slam.

"We have to get the *hell* out of here." Harry rushes to the truck, sticks half his body into the cabin and rummages around. He returns holding two plastic bags. He gives one to Travis.

"*Clean it up*," he says.

Travis does as he's told, and they both crawl on the ground picking up all the chunks of the gnome. Harry grabs the torso, which is still gesturing up towards the sky, and shakes his head sadly. He looks towards Travis. "Two hundred goddamn years old."

They drive away from the scene of the crime, and Harry says, without taking the eyes off the road, "I don't want to be tied up in this." He can't stop shaking his head. "I'm gonna drop you off at home. You are gonna bring the gnome inside. You're gonna take that bereavement they wanted you to take."

"I'm not taking leave, man."

"*You are taking the goddamn bereavement*," Harry hisses. "You are going to figure out how to *fix this*. Because, I got nothing. No ideas. I just know I don't want any part of it."

"I'm not taking leave," Travis repeats.

Harry slams the truck to a squealing halt. "If you don't take some goddamn time off, I'm going to tell everyone in Ruckus about what you did. You'll have to move, kid. I'm not sure if there's an ending to this where you *don't* have to move. I have half a mind to run you out of town myself. But I'm not gonna. I'm gonna drop you off at home. You're gonna call the station. You're gonna take some time off. You're gonna figure out why the hell you kicked that gnome's head off."

***

It's five days into Travis's bereavement, and he's drunk. His boss had been understanding. He had sounded pleased when Travis called him. He told Travis he should not take a week. He should take the whole month. "Have a wonderful Christmas," he'd said over the phone.

So, if Travis was being made to bereave, he bereaved in the only way he knew how. He went to The Worthington Room every night and drank vodka cranberries. When he returned to his apartment each night, only a few blocks from Main Street, the two bags of gnome greeted him from his dining room table.

"Has anyone been able to find it yet?" Travis hears from down the bar. "I came up here with the family from Davenport for the weekend. It's not supposed to be this hard to find, right?"

The bartender shrugs at the gnome hunter. "I've been on the lookout too. I found this cow about a month ago, like a wooden cow about yay big," he extends his arms out in front of him two feet apart, "and when I find the gnome I'm gonna set them out in front of the bar so it looks like he and the cow are, you know..."

The customer scrunches his face in disgust at the bartender. "That's disgusting."

The bartender shrugs again and walks down towards Travis. "What do you think, Travis?"

"'Bout what?" he asks, after taking a long drag from his beer.

"Where's the gnome gone?"

"I don't *know*. It's crazy that anybody even... why does it even matter?"

The bartender grabs Travis' empty glass and goes to refill it. "It's kind of our whole thing."

When Travis leaves the bar, he walks behind a small family: a woman with her hood up and two small kids. He can't make out what they're saying, but he knows that they're searching for the Ruckus gnome. Everyone is searching.

He sees a glove drop from one of the kids' jacket pocket. He picks up speed, scoops the glove up, and catches up with the family. He's holding the glove out in front of him when he says, "Excuse me, you dropped this."

The three turn and he jolts to a stop.

"Uncle Travis!" both Lochlin and Richard exclaim in unison. They both hug one leg each.

Travis looks up, makes eye contact with Lydia. He can tell that she feels as awkward as he does.

"Hey Travis," she manages.

"Hey Lydia," he says. He bends down so that he's eye level with the two boys. "Hey guys."

"We haven't seen you in *so* long," says Lochlin.

"That's not true. I saw you..." he looks up, trying to think. He sees Lydia staring at him from the corner of his eye. "Well, I guess it has been a while. I'm sorry. We'll have to hang soon."

He stands.

"Well, we're looking for that gnome now," Richard says. "You can help us."

Travis looks to Lydia for help. She remains silent. "I don't know guys. I heard he's super hard to find this year. You might just want to get some hot chocolate and watch some TV tonight."

"You're telling them to give up?"

Travis is taken aback by Lydia's sudden shift in tone. She's staring daggers into him.

"I…"

"You don't have to come with us, Travis," says Lydia with a snip. "But we're going to keep looking."

He gapes, sheepishly. "Yeah. Yeah. Of course."

"Because we don't give up," says Lydia.

"I know."

"Because giving up is stupid."

"We're not allowed to say stupid," Richard reminds his mother.

"Yes, we are honey. When something is really stupid, we can call it stupid."

Richard looks towards his brother, his eyes filled with wonder at this newfound knowledge.

"You always used to brag about how good you were at finding the gnome when you were a kid," Lydia reminds Travis. "You can come. You don't have to just…" she trails off.

"I…," says Travis, looking at his feet. "I have something I have to take care of."

When Travis walks into his cluttered apartment that night, he heads to the refrigerator. Attached to the door by a magnet is a photograph of him and his older brother Hayden when they were younger. In the picture, they're both bundled up in winter coats and between them, stuck in a bush in front of Clarence Veterinarian on University Avenue is the gnome.

Travis can remember the argument he and Hayden had gotten into after they'd found it. Hayden wanted to put it on a roof of a building on Main Street. Travis wanted to hide it in the sewer to try and bait crocodiles with it.

Travis takes the photo and sits down at his dining room table in front of the bags of broken gnome. He studies what it once looked like, before its head was fragments. He grabs two pieces from the bag. They're both chunks of face.

Travis brings them both up together so they're touching.

The pieces don't fit right.

They're incongruous.

***

The next morning, Travis makes the five-minute walk to his parent's house from his apartment. His mother opens the door and smiles when she sees her son's face. "You don't write. You don't call."

He stands in the living room. All around there are photographs of Travis and Hayden, different accolades they'd received in school. More numerous than anything else, though, are tiny little sculptures. Finely crafted things consisting of bent wire, metal, and wood, all constructed by Travis's brother.

The TV's on and he watches the news as his mom makes coffee in the kitchen. The mayor of Ruckus is on the television. He's talking about the Christmas season, and the time-honored tradition of the Ruckus gnome. The newscast cuts to footage of children walking up and down Main Street, searching.

"And remember," the mayor says from the television. "Once you find the gnome, try not to hide it in an impossible-to-find spot. That can really ruin the fun for everyone." His eyes are pleading into the camera when he says this.

"I don't think this has ever happened," says Travis' mom, standing in the doorway of the dining room holding two cups of coffee. "They've always found it by now. You and Hayden certainly would have."

Travis looks towards his mom. Next to her, hung on the wall, is a photograph of him and Hayden as adults on a camping trip in Washington. They're both holding massive trout in the picture.

"What?" Travis asks. His eyes linger on the photograph.

"I can't believe it's taken this long into the month to find the gnome," says his mom setting the coffee cups on the coffee table. "They're even talkin' about it at church."

"I guess I didn't realize that it was such a big deal," says Travis.

"You didn't realize that it was such a big deal?" says his mother, sitting down on the sofa and sliding one of the mugs towards her son. "You and your brother used to go crazy for that gnome." She smiles at the memory.

Travis sits across from her on a white chair.

"Yeah," he says. "But it's not just kids. It's the mayor. This guy at the bar said he'd travelled far just to see it. I feel like I don't hear about it usually. It's just a thing that happens, and nobody talks about it. But now everyone's talking about it."

His mother shrugs. "Maybe if you had some kids, you'd understand."

"*Jesus* mom."

"Speaking of kids. Did you get my text? Lydia and the boys are coming over tonight for dinner with your father and me. I'm sure they'd love to see you."

Travis makes himself sink lower in the chair. "I don't know. I think I have stuff going on."

His mother pauses for a moment, seems to be caught in a thought. "I wasn't going to say anything. I was going to let you say something. But you don't seem to be saying anything, so I'll say something. Your father saw Gary Hutchins at the grocery store. He told him that you have the whole month off for bereavement?"

Travis sinks as fully into the chair as possible.

"And I think that's great sweetie. I think it's necessary and something you should do. Though, you *smell* like the bar."

Travis shuts his eyes as if that will make his mother's voice go away.

"I'm just a little curious," she continues. "Why now? Why six months later?"

They hear the front door open and then close. Travis' dad enters the room holding groceries. His face lights up when he sees him.

"My son!" he says. "How's vacation?"

"It's not va*cation,* Doug," Travis's mom insists.

"Are you coming to dinner?" he ignores his wife.

"I was just telling mom. I think I have something going on."

"You don't have anything going on," says his father. "It'll be fun. We're going gnome hunting after. We're going to find that crafty little bastard."

Travis covers his face with his hands and groans.

"What's wrong?"

"Nothing," says Travis. It comes muffled from behind his fingers. "Maybe I'll come to dinner."

"Great!"

"Maybe."

Before he leaves, Travis asks his dad to see the wheelless Firebird that's been sitting in the garage for years now. His dad leads him to the garage and they both stare at the orange car in silence.

"Why'd uh...," his dad starts. "Why'd you wanna see it? You've never cared about this thing."

"How can you stand it?" Travis blurts out.

"What?"

"Seeing them. Richard and Lochlin."

"My grandchildren?"

"Yes. How can you bring yourself to look at their faces."

"They're cute faces."

"They just look... you know what I'm saying. They look just like... they act just like... they talk like him, dad. They're just like him."

His father frowns. "Why the hell would that make me not want to see them?"

"Because..." Travis throws his arms up in frustration. "Because it really really hurts me. Seeing them. It makes me remember that, he's just... he's not here anymore. And all of this talk about that *stupid* gnome. It's all like, too much."

"Stupid gnome?"

"Yes, the stupid gnome."

"You boys love that gnome."

"*Loved,* dad. *Loved.* Then we grew up. Some of us fucking *di*ed."

His father's shoulders sag.

"I'm sorry. I'm sorry," says Travis contritely. "It's just... how are people not... what is the deal with this gnome?"

His father thinks for a moment. "It's a tradition," he finally says. "It's important. Come to dinner."

***

Strewn about on the floor of Travis's apartment are all the pieces of the gnome. He's laid them out on a sheet and organized them based on where they might go in relation to the gnome's head. At the top of the sheet are chunks of red hat. On the bottom are pieces of his beard. Off to the left and right are his eyes and the back of his head. His ears. And in the center of all of it is his torso with his hand lifted above his decapitated body.

On the way home Travis had stopped at the hardware store to buy carpenter's glue. Now, he stands above the sheet and stares at the mishmash that he's created for himself. He runs his fingers through his hair. He gets down on his knees and in one hand picks up the gnome's eye and in the other a chunk of flesh-colored clay. He places them together. He wiggles them around trying to get them to fit together.

They don't fit.

He throws them to the corners of the room. His eyes drift to the refrigerator, to the picture of him and his big brother with the gnome in between them. He sees their smiles. His eyes drift upwards. On top of the refrigerator is one of Hayden's sculptures. A tiny elephant made of twisted wire. Travis smiles glumly at the elephant.

***

There's a knock on the door. Travis is still seated in front of the sheet. He stands up, walks slowly to the door. He looks through the peephole.

His father stands there, looking down at his feet. He wears a checkered button up.

Travis cracks the door open enough so the two can see each other.

"I don't think I'm coming to dinner."

"Travis."

"Dad, I don't feel well. Okay? I just don't feel great."

"Can I come in?"

Travis looks over his shoulder, at the splintered gnome. "Now's really not a great time."

"Is someone in there?"

"No."

"Do you have a lady over?" His dad pushes the door, but it is stopped by Travis' foot.

"No!" cries Travis.

His father pushes the door open with his shoulder. His strength surprises Travis, and he opens the door wide enough for him to see the mess within the apartment.

"What is that?" he asks.

Travis relents. He backs away his foot, and his father enters the apartment.

"Is that…"

"Yes."

"Dear lord," His father says. He approaches the sheet and lowers himself down to get closer to the pieces of the gnome. "What the hell happened?"

"I was on my route. And I saw it, and it just totally startled m…" Travis says, trailing off. He stands there, staring at his father.

"It startled you? And you destroyed it?"

Travis takes a deep breath. "It pissed me off. It pissed me off seeing it there, smiling like normal. Like it's any other December. It pissed me off, and I kicked it, Dad."

His father lifts Travis's handiwork and examines it. In the past few hours, all Travis has managed to do is shoddily glue together a few mismatched pieces to each other. It looks nothing like the gnome in the picture on the refrigerator. The eyes are lopsided. The nose is off center. The smile is crooked.

His dad turns from the demented gnome to look at his son. "I hate it too."

"What?"

"I hate acting like everything's normal. I really, really hate it."

His dad stands and closes the distance between them. "Seeing those boys does sting a little. They have his eyes. They laugh just like he used to laugh." He puts a hand on Travis's shoulder. "Everything's not normal. Your mom and I cry most nights. We cry hard. But we do it together. We're with each other. And yes, it stings to see those kids. But it feels good, too. It feels so much better than it stings. It's amazing that he left pieces of himself scattered around the world for us to see and smile at."

There's tears in Travis's eyes. He hangs his head low, taking tiny breaths. "I just miss him, Dad."

"And whether or not you come to dinner won't change that."

Travis nods. He nods, keeps taking tiny breaths.

"You're not gonna be able to fix it like that," his dad says, indicating the deformed, glued-together gnome face.

"How do I fix it?"

"You've got to make a new head."

Travis, despite himself, manages a laugh. "I can't do that. That's impossible."

His father looks at him, a serious expression on his face. "It's absolutely not impossible. Somebody made it, way back when. Besides. It's in your blood."

***

It's December 15th. Nobody in the town has found the gnome. Despite this, families wander around Main Street laughing and wandering about; enjoying each other's joy.

Travis walks down the street with his parents, Lydia, and her two boys.

"Thank you for coming Travis," Lydia had whispered to him after they'd all met up at his parent's house.

Richard and Lochlin had both screamed in delight when they saw him. "Uncle Travis!" they'd said in unison.

Now, they walk down Main Street sipping on hot chocolates.

"Are we looking for the gnome still?" asks Lochlin. "It's gotta be around here somewhere."

"Nobody's ever gonna find it," says Richard. "It's never been this hard before."

Travis and his father share a look. Travis walks out ahead of the group, bends down so he's eye level with the two boys.

"It's around here somewhere," he says. "You know, your dad and I wanted to give up, a long time ago. We walked around for hours looking for the gnome. We thought it was impossible too."

"But you found it?" Lochlin asks.

"We found it."

Above them, on the roof of Lincoln's Savings Bank LLC, is the gnome. It's placed on the very edge of the building, clearly visible to anyone who decides to look up. It looks different than it has for the past two hundred years. Its beard is shorter. Its eyes are painted green instead of blue. Its hat is orange. The color of its face does not match that of its hands.

But still, with one of its arms it gestures up to the sky.

Check this out. Isn't this great?

***

About the Author

Cole Thorna was born and raised in Upstate New York. He decided to move to the cornfields of Iowa in July of 2019. Since then he's cooked countless hamburgers, learned how to drive, and, most recently, enrolled at University of Iowa where he is studying English and Creative Writing.

4

THE BEST WORST CHRISTMAS EVER

By Melinda Wichmann

Friday, Dec. 22

If I needed proof this was going to be the worst Christmas ever, I didn't have to look any further than the sign looming in my SUV's windshield as I slowed for the city limits.

Welcome to Ridge, Population 2,047
Home of the Fighting Bobcats!

A snarling bobcat caricature swatted at the star designating Ridge's location in east central Iowa. The little farming town didn't even merit an adjective like Smuggler's Ridge or Meteor Ridge or anything that would entice travelers to pull off I-80 for a visit.

But here I was, Laurel Hansen, coming to you live from possibly the dullest place on earth.

Three days before Christmas.

Alone.

I was here of my own free will, sort of, which made it even worse. The Hansen family Christmas had been canceled this year because everybody—except me—had gone and made big, happy plans. Granted, my folks *had* invited me to accompany them to visit Mom's sister in Arizona for the holidays. That sounded good on the surface, but Aunt Carla has strong opinions on politics, cats, and why I'm still single at twenty-eight. I'm sure she'd have one on why I'm unemployed, too. I took a hard pass.

My older sister, Jen, suggested I join her family on their Disney cruise, like I had that kind of money just laying around. No job, remember? Besides, I doubted the amount of alcohol available on a Disney cruise would be sufficient to ease the current mess of my life, and I didn't want my nieces thinking Auntie Laurel was a lush.

Little sister Amy and her fiancé bravely asked me to come with them on their ski trip to Aspen. Ditto about the money, but mostly I had zero desire to be a third wheel while they walked down candlelit streets, holding hands and gazing at one another in the falling snow.

And just forget an intimate holiday for two with Adam. He couldn't break up with me fast enough after my on-air disaster, like guilt by association would tarnish his own rising broadcast career.

Nope, I'd just hide in my apartment, sending out resumés and hoping no one recognized me when I made a Target run for wine and chocolate. I was a grown-ass adult. I could be alone at Christmas. No big deal. Really.

Then Jen put on her bossy pants and decided I should clean out Great-aunt Jo's house at Ridge.

"Isn't that *your* job? Jo named you the executor of her estate, not me," I protested.

"That house needs to be cleaned out so I can sell it. Jo was a tidy housekeeper, I'm sure it'll only take a week or two." Jen's annoying mom-practicality came through the phone loud and clear. "It's not like you have anything else to do."

Ouch.

As I turned off the gravel road into my great-aunt and -uncle's farm lane, I reluctantly admitted the snowfall that had plagued me since Grinnell, combined with the winter twilight, made the big Victorian farmhouse look like a Hallmark card. A wave of nostalgia rolled over me as I remembered the Christmases I spent here when Jen, Amy, and I were in elementary school. Great-aunt Jo, my grandpa's sister, and her husband Ed didn't have kids, but their home was the epicenter for family holidays. Those get-togethers were everything Christmas should be—the aroma of roasting ham filling the house and all my aunts, uncles, and cousins arriving with favorite side dishes and brightly wrapped packages.

Ed cut a red cedar tree from the river bottom every year. It was usually lopsided and shaggy, but it filled the bay window where it sparkled with tinsel and lights and Jo's collection of antique glass ornaments. Those ornaments were a wedding gift, sent from a relative in Norway, and Jen, Amy, and I were *not*, under any circumstances, to touch them or Santa wouldn't come. The spun glass balls were so beautiful I was sure they were magical, and if I could hold one in my hands and make a wish, it would come true. But the threat of Santa not stopping was serious business, so I kept my little hands to myself.

We stopped making the Christmas trek from our farm near Clear Lake to Jo and Ed's on the other side of the state when my sisters and I were in high school. Life got crazy with school and sports and 4-H, and my parents decided we would have Christmas at home instead. Ed died five years ago, and Jo lived alone until failing health sent her to a care center for the last few months of her life. She was ninety-one when she passed in late November. I didn't go to her funeral. That was the week I got fired.

I wrenched myself back to the present. Jen assured me the farm tenant, a guy who rented the barn and pastureland for a cow/calf operation, knew I was coming. He had a key to the house and would plug in the refrigerator and turn up the furnace. His contact info was on Jen's carefully scripted to-do list. In addition to cleaning out the house, I was to arrange to have the HVAC serviced, hire a junk hauler, find local charities taking household goods, and contact area antique dealers. I'd only given the list a cursory glance before stuffing it in my bag, still bitter Jen would be spending Christmas floating around in the Caribbean while I was trying to avoid frostbite in Ridge.

I parked in front of the house and got out of my car. That's when the yelling started.

"Cake! Get the cake!" someone shouted in a tone that indicated pending disaster.

I looked around for a cake in need of rescue but saw only a man on a John Deere loader tractor driving as fast as traction allowed in the cattle lot near the barn. Moving forward with single-minded determination at a ninety-degree angle were half a dozen Black Angus cows. The goal of both parties was an open gate. It was clear who was going to get there first.

"Cake!" the man yelled again, pointing emphatically. Grasping the context of the situation, I realized he was saying "Gate!"

I bolted through the snow, waving my arms at the approaching beasts to turn them back. Twenty feet away, the cows' fourteen-hundred-pound bodies gained speed at the scent of pending freedom.

I threw myself into the open gateway. "Git back! Git! Back! Haaaaa!" I flapped my arms and hoped I looked sufficiently threatening. It had been a hot minute since I'd watched gates for my dad as he chored. Now my world was ruled by deadlines, on-camera wardrobe and studio makeup. At least it had been.

The cows stopped and snorted, eyeing me with suspicion. Gratified, I walked forward, arms outstretched, making loud references to hamburger. Stock cows, even en masse, are not that brave. In the face of this human impediment, they reversed course and lumbered back toward the barn.

The roar of the tractor engine running wide open grew louder. I stepped out of the way as the driver roared through the opening, then I drug the steel, five-bar gate shut behind him. The man stopped the tractor and killed the engine.

"Can't thank you enough for that!" he said, jumping down.

I turned from hooking the chain welded to the gate around a thick wooden post and looked up into a face with a square jaw and long, straight nose. And I mean *looked up*. This guy was tall. He was about my age, with a lean build and broad shoulders. An ear-to-ear smile lit up his face. He pulled off a glove and extended his hand. "Tyler Andersen."

"Laurel Hansen, Jo's great-niece." I shook his hand, praying he wouldn't recognize me. Ridge was hundreds of miles away from the Twin Cities market of my broadcast station—former broadcast station—but footage of the incident had gone viral, taking my career with it.

Tyler gestured to a harvested corn field south of the barn. "I just moved these cows up to the barn because the weather's supposed to turn bad, but all they want to do is get back out there." He shook his head. "Thought I could drop hay without shutting that gate. Thanks again. You save me one big headache."

"Nobody wants to chase black cows in the dark," I said, relaxing as he showed no sign of identifying me as anyone other than Jo's niece. "You mentioned the weather—how bad is bad?"

"Heavy snow, blizzard conditions. Starting on Christmas Eve day."

I forced a professional smile and tried to look like being alone during a raging winter storm was every girl's Christmas wish. I looked around, taking in mounds of snow already pushed to the perimeter of the barnyard from today's storm. "Thanks for plowing the lane for me."

"No problem. I'll be back in the morning to finish clearing around the buildings." He gestured toward the house. "I can go in with you if you want."

"Thanks, but I spent a lot of time here when I was a kid. I'll be fine," I said with more confidence than I felt.

"See you later then." Tyler parked the tractor in the machine shed and rolled the door shut. I was pulling luggage out of my car as he drove down the lane in an old Chevy pickup. He waved, and I waved back. I stood for a minute in the twilight, breathing in the cold air and the earthy scent of cows. Then the silence was broken by the yapping howls of coyotes in the near distance, and I turned toward the house.

Tyler had thoughtfully shoveled a path to the back door. I carried my supplies onto the porch, feeling like an explorer who'd just been dropped into the wilderness. The sleeping bag and pillow, duffel loaded with sensible winter clothes, and cooler packed with perishables huddled at my feet as I slid the key in the lock. The back door swung open without protest, and I was met by a welcome gust of warm air. For a second, I smelled roasting ham underlaid by the tang of fresh cut cedar and a crackling wood fire. The memory faded as quickly as it came, replaced by the dusty, tired scent old houses get when no one lives there anymore. I fumbled for the kitchen light switch.

Oh. Holy. Hell.

The level of clutter was staggering. Jo's pristine housekeeping had vanished with the days of our Norman Rockwell family gatherings, and she'd become a Grade A packrat as she aged. The kitchen table was piled high with mail-order catalogs, jigsaw puzzle boxes, and faded fliers advertising long-past church soup suppers. Once tidy countertops were a haphazard collection of everything from silk flowers stuffed in mason jars to stacks of foam cold-drink cups from Casey's. Overflowing bags of old clothes and stacks of books marched along the walls and disappeared into the butler's pantry.

I walked through the house with increasing dismay. Every flat surface was piled high, including the beds in all four bedrooms and most of the floor space. It wasn't going to take a week to clean out the house. It was going to take a week to clean out one room, and that was if an avalanche of accumulated stuff didn't fall over and kill me first. The thirty-two-count box of contractor grade trash bags I brought suddenly did not seem up to the task. I considered calling Jen to express my feelings, but decided not to. I hoped a fish bit her on the butt when she was snorkeling.

Returning to the kitchen, my eyes took in details my brain had been too overwhelmed to notice earlier. Someone had made a valiant attempt to clear part of the counter, and a Tupperware container sat in the conquered space. A note taped to the lid read "Merry Christmas, from Kathy." I pried it open. The scent of sugar and chocolate wafted upward from a sampling of holiday treats. Suddenly ravenous, I helped myself. Buttercream frosting melted in my mouth as the sweet almond and vanilla flavor of a cookie filled my senses. God bless Kathy. She must be Tyler's wife.

When I opened the refrigerator to put away the food I'd brought, I found a bag of ground coffee, a bowl of homemade fruit salad, and a dozen brown eggs on the middle shelf. The attached note read, "Enjoy. Please let us know if you need anything. Tell Ty." Again, it was signed "Kathy." I might spend Christmas alone, but I wouldn't spend it hungry.

I made a sandwich with the cold-cuts I'd brought, helped myself to the fruit salad and, after a minor search, unearthed the remote to Jo's hulking television set. The meteorologist on the six p.m. news cheerfully predicted Santa would need Rudolph to guide his sleigh this year since a major winter storm would hit the area on Christmas Eve.

I had a sudden, vivid memory of sitting in this room as a child, watching "Rudolph the Red Nosed Reindeer," narrated by Burl Ives, with Jen and Amy while the glass ornaments on the Christmas tree sparkled. I'd been seven years old that year, and we'd watched the stop-action animated adventures of Rudolph and Hermey and the Abominable Snow Monster with delight. Amy, then five, had been terrified of the Abominable, so Jen and I spent the entire holiday telling her it lived in the barn.

I laughed at the memory. Fine. If I had to spend Christmas with nothing but memories for company, at least they were happy ones. After a few hours of tentatively poking around in the kitchen, I shoveled off the couch, which had less stuff piled on it than any of the beds, unrolled my sleeping bag and called it a day.

Saturday, Dec. 23

I'd coaxed Jo's industrial size coffee maker to life when Tyler Andersen arrived just after sunrise. I watched as he maneuvered the tractor and its attached snow blade as if executing a military drill. He cleared access to the barn, garage and outbuildings in short order.

I was wondering what I was going to do with twelve cups of coffee—the obvious answer was a little extreme, even for me—when he knocked on the back door.

"My mom sent this for you." He held out a foil-covered, baking dish. "Hope you like tater tot casserole."

I liked anything I didn't have to cook myself. "Please tell her thank you," I said. "And tell your wife thanks for the cookies and the food in the fridge."

"My—no—I'm not married. Kathy's my mom. She found out you were coming, and she likes to feed people."

"Would you like to come in for coffee?" It was the most Norwegian, Lutheran thing I could have said, and we both recognized it at the same time. Ty's resulting smile was worth a moment's appreciation. Recovering, I said, "I had to make an entire pot just to get the coffee maker to come on. If I drink it all, I'll be climbing the walls. Come in and save me from myself."

"Since you put it that way." He toed off his chore boots on the porch before ducking through the kitchen door. The response must have been automatic. He was at least six-four. He unzipped his heavy jacket to reveal insulated bibs over a hooded sweatshirt over a flannel shirt. It was the winter farm uniform I'd grown up with, and it made Jo's kitchen feel less like a disaster area and more like home.

"Have a seat. If you can find one." I shoved a shoe box filled with grocery store coupons and a pile of ancient newspapers further into the mess on the table and was relieved when nothing fell off the other end. I poured coffee into two mugs and set the box of cookies on the table.

"How long are you here for?" Ty asked, helping himself.

"The original plan was a couple of weeks, but there's no way I'll get this cleaned out that fast. Jen—my sister—wants to sell the place as soon as she can. Old houses that sit empty are trouble waiting to happen, especially in winter."

"I don't mind keeping an eye on it. I'm over here every day to check cows."

"Thanks, but all this stuff has to be dealt with. I don't know how long that will take." I stopped before adding, *it's not like I have anything else to do.*

"You look really familiar," Ty said. "I feel like I've seen you before."

I cringed inwardly. Here it came. The ten seconds of fame I couldn't escape.

He snapped his fingers. "That's it. You look like a younger version of Jo. Seriously, you do. She must have been really good looking when she was—" He stopped. "I don't mean you're—I did mean—you *are* pretty—oh, hell."

I bit the inside of my cheek to keep from smiling as color rose in his cheeks. His sheepish grin was a mile wide and made more attractive by a slightly crooked front tooth.

"Well, I've stuck my foot in it. Time to go. Thanks." He drained his mug and stood, then asked. "Is your family coming here for Christmas?"

"No."

"Are you going anywhere?"

"No. My family all went in different directions this year. It's okay." If I said that often enough, maybe I'd start believing it. Courtesy dictated I return the question. "Does your family do a big holiday thing?"

Ty rolled his eyes. "My brother and his wife are having family over tonight to celebrate my niece's first birthday. Then we have Christmas Eve at my folks', and on Christmas Day, we go to my aunt and uncle's in town. By the twenty-sixth, I'll be in a food coma and won't know what day it is." He sobered. "Call me if you need anything. My place is on the highway, just a few miles south."

"I'll be fine," I said, envious of his family-based Christmas itinerary but determined not to show it. "The fridge is full, the furnace is working, and I've got plenty to do."

"Have a merry Christmas!" he said.

"You, too." My attempt at holiday cheer rang hollow, but he didn't seem to notice.

After he left, I turned on the radio by the sink. The dial was set to WMT, Cedar Rapids, like it had always been when Jo and Ed were alive. Twenty minutes later, I'd learned corn prices were down, fat cattle were selling for $230 per hundred weight, and the National Weather Service had issued a winter storm watch for eastern Iowa on Christmas Eve. Joy to the world.

By six p.m., I'd logged eleven dusty hours of sorting, tossing, and boxing but hadn't gotten further than cleaning off the kitchen table and dealing with the archaeological dig on the countertops. I heated Kathy Andersen's casserole and watched "A Charlie Brown Christmas." By nine p.m., I was asleep with visions of boxes labeled *Burn, Donate,* and *Keep* dancing in my head. So much for sugarplums.

Sunday, Dec. 24

I spent the day emptying cupboards impacted with seven decades of kitchen things, including an impressive collection of harvest gold and avocado green Tupperware. When I stumbled over the worn cardboard box labeled *Christmas Decorations* in the butler's pantry, I decided it was quitting time. It was Christmas Eve, after all, and maybe wallowing in the nostalgia of décor from my childhood would lift my spirits. It would be a delight to find those glass ornaments that sparkled so brightly in all my holiday memories. What were the odds they'd actually be in a box marked *Christmas Decorations*?

WMT was playing Christmas carols and giving forecasts. The National Weather Service had upgraded the earlier watch to a winter storm warning and added a blizzard warning for good measure. Eight to ten inches of snow would be accompanied by thirty mile an hour winds and white-out conditions. Outside the snow-crusted windows, not a creature was stirring. I imagined the cows, snug in the lower level of the barn, sheltered from the elements by thick limestone walls. Ty had been here in the early afternoon, setting thousand-pound round bales of hay into metal ring feeders for the herd. I'd cheerfully abandoned the kitchen clutter and gone out to watch gates so he didn't have to climb off and on the tractor repeatedly. We spoke briefly, but with snow and wind setting in, he didn't linger.

I sorted through the box of decorations with a sinking heart. Time and the occasional mouse had taken their toll. Tinsel garlands were tarnished with age, and the strings of vintage lights would probably set a tree on fire in about five minutes. Even the gold foil star that gleamed from the treetop in my memories was dull and bent. Holding my breath, I lifted out a yellowed box with Armstrong's Department Store, Cedar Rapids, Iowa, embossed on the lid. It held only a collection of quilted fabric decorations, the once bright cloth now faded.

I sighed with disappointment. It had been silly to think I'd find the glass ornaments. They were so fragile, they might not have survived the years. Or Jo could have donated them to a church rummage sale or gifted them to a friend. I saved the quilted decorations for Jen and Amy and tossed the rest of the junk back in the box.

The sound of a revving engine sent me to the window to see Ty's pickup plowing through the deepening drifts in the lane. When I opened the back door, he handed me a backpack and an enormous wicker picnic basket.

"I'll be back in a minute." Without waiting, he climbed in his truck and drove to the barn, where his snow-blurred silhouette vanished inside.

I hung the backpack on a chair and opened the basket. It held a small Crockpot filled with cocktail sausages swimming in barbecue sauce, flour-dusted dinner rolls that had to be homemade, a bowl of broccoli and grape salad, and an entire pecan pie. Kathy must think I was an emaciated waif from a Dickens novel.

The sound of boots stomping off snow on the porch heralded Ty's return. It was full dark now, the snow a billowing curtain against the glow of the security light between house and barn.

"What are you doing out here? The roads must be awful," I said as he ducked into the kitchen.

"They are. I had to check that tank heater and plug in the block heater on the tractor or it won't start tomorrow." He shuffled awkwardly and looked anywhere but at me. I swore the color in his cheeks was due to more than the cold. Finally, he said, "When the temperature drops, those drifts are going to freeze into cement. Can I, uh, stay here tonight? I'm afraid I won't be able to get here to check cows tomorrow, and I don't trust that tank heater to stay on. If you're not okay with it, just tell me. But I brought supper. And my own toothbrush." His grin was irrepressible.

"Of course you can stay," I said. Iowa nice and the desperate need not to be alone on Christmas Eve had me inviting a guy I barely knew to a slumber party of two. "But you'll miss your family get-together."

"No, I won't," he said. "Everyone except me and my one-year-old-niece is barfing their guts out."

I stared. "What?"

"Melissa, that's my brother's wife, made clam chowder for the party yesterday." He made a face. "Apparently the clams were past their prime. This morning, everyone who had the soup was heaving. I can't stand clams in the first place, so I'm okay."

He waved at the containers on the table. "This is the food my mom had already fixed for tonight. She called and told me to come get it because neither she nor Dad could stand to look at it. The Andersen family Christmas is officially canceled."

"I am so sorry," I said. "Didn't she want to keep any of it?"

"She couldn't get it out of the house fast enough. She thinks by tomorrow they might be up for crackers and chicken broth. I figured if I showed up on your doorstep with all this food, you'd have to let me stay."

***

We filled plates and watched "Home Alone," which is even funnier when you aren't actually home alone. The thermometer in the kitchen showed the outdoor temp had dropped to eight degrees above zero, and the world beyond the windows was an abyss of swirling white. When it was time to turn in, I told Ty he should take the couch.

"You're too tall for the recliner. You won't get any sleep, and you'll be cranky in the morning, and I'm not going to be snowed in with a cranky farmer," I said. "Let me find you a pillow and some blankets."

I jogged up the stairs to the linen cupboard on the second floor. The door swung open to reveal shelves jammed with blankets, quilts, pillows, a collection of hats, a box labeled *Veterinary Syringes*, a bundle of marshmallow roasting forks, a bag of what might be old pantyhose, and a vintage Remington typewriter.

"The entire house is like this," I said to Ty, who'd followed me. "If Jen wants it completely cleaned out, I'll be here until spring."

"Don't you have a job to go back to?" he asked.

"Not anymore."

"What happened?" His straightforward curiosity took any sting out of the question.

"I was a reporter for a TV station in the Twin Cities. I said some inappropriate things on-camera."

"What kind of inappropriate things?"

"Four-letter ones. The kind that get you fired," I said darkly. "You're nosey."

"If you'd been fired because you threatened to kill your boss, I might change my mind about staying here tonight."

I laughed in spite of myself. "I was doing a live outdoor weather segment during a snowstorm when a guy lost control of his car. He sideswiped my camera operator and knocked both of us into a ditch. The techs at the studio were convinced we'd both been killed, and they mishandled the delay so the entire Twin Cities heard me screaming...um...words. Not my proudest moment."

"Did the police arrest the driver?"

"Sort of. The guy had just moved here from Florida. He had no clue how to drive in an inch of snow, let alone six. He got fined, and I got fired for unprofessional conduct."

"Maybe it was a sign you should try another career path."

"Like what? Opening a driving school for non-Midwesterners?"

Ty laughed, but I wondered if he was right. Maybe the whole mess was the universe telling me to do something different.

"Our local newspaper is always short-staffed. I could put in a good word for you. My sister-in-law is the editor."

"The sister-in-law who just poisoned your entire family?"

He shrugged. "She writes better than she cooks."

I tugged a pillow and blanket off the shelf at eye level, which is the only reason I saw the box. It was wrapped in dusty brown kraft paper tied with string, and for a second, I heard Jo singing the Julie Andrews classic "My Favorite Things." I shoved the pillow and blanket into Ty's chest. He caught them with good grace and looked over my shoulder as I pulled the box into the light. *Laurel* was written in Jo's neat script on a small envelope tucked under the string.

"What is it?" Ty asked.

"Probably a Barbie doll," I said, imagining a gift my great-aunt had stashed away for a Christmas twenty years ago and forgotten about. I carried it down to the living room. Ty sat on the edge of the couch, his elbows on his knees. "What are you waiting for? Open it!"

"You're like a little kid," I said, enjoying his enthusiasm. "It can't be a Christmas present. It's not even wrapped in Christmas paper."

"It's a present, and it's Christmas Eve, so it's a Christmas present," Ty said.

I opened the envelope and pulled out a sheet of pale blue stationery. My eyes misted at the familiar handwriting.

My dearest Laurel – I know this will find you eventually. I hope it brings you as much joy as it did me and may each of your Christmases be more blessed than the one before. Great-Aunt Jo. It was dated July 2025, one month before she went into the care center and four months before her death.

The string fell away easily when I tugged at the bow knot. I hesitated, unsure how to tackle the paper, which didn't have any visible seams.

"Please don't tell me you save wrapping paper and reuse it," Ty said. "Just rip it off."

I smiled at him and slowly picked at a piece of tape.

"You're killing me," he groaned.

I got a hand under the paper and yanked. It came off in one sheet, revealing a box adorned with a picture of a 1970s orange Rival Crockpot. I unfolded the cardboard flaps. As advertised, the slow cooker nestled amid sheets of crumpled newsprint. Shaking my head, I tipped the box to show Ty. "Aunt Jo did love her Crockpot. She probably boxed up her electric skillet and the toaster for Jen and Amy."

He pointed at the glass lid. "What's that? Under there."

"Just more packing—oh—wait." I lifted the lid and pulled out another wad of newspaper. The appliance's ceramic liner was full of what looked like over-sized golf balls, each swaddled in tissue. I unwrapped one and stared in disbelief.

"What is it?" Ty looked at me, not my hands.

I swallowed hard. "The glass ornaments she hung on the tree every year. When I was little, I thought they were magic, that if I held one and made a wish, it would come true." I tipped my palm to show him, and red glass, fragile as a soap bubble, sparkled in the light.

"You should make a wish now," Ty said. "It's Christmas Eve, it has to come true."

I looked around the room, at the jumble of Jo and Ed's lives. I looked at Ty, sprawled on the couch, all legs and feet and intriguing smile. The cloud of self-conscious frustration that plagued me for the last month started to lift. Maybe Jen's marching orders to clear out the basement-to-attic clutter of this place was a gift in disguise. There was no rush to find a new broadcast job and step back into the forced on-camera professionalism I wasn't sure I was cut out for. I could spend months here, clearing out this house, rediscovering family treasures and reliving memories. That would give me time to decide what I wanted to do. I re-wrapped the glass ball in its cocoon of tissue paper.

"It already has," I said.

The tips of Ty's ears turned red, but his gray eyes rested steadily on mine, and a rush of warmth rippled through me.

"Merry Christmas, Laurel," he said.

"Merry Christmas, Ty." This time, I meant it.

***

About the Author

Melinda Wichmann is a third-generation farm kid who earned a journalism degree from Iowa State University and spent thirty-five years living the dream in eastern Iowa community newspapers. She and her husband, also a third-generation farm kid, live near the Amana Colonies, where she is a master at watching gates and woefully inadequate at chasing loose cows. Her first novel, "How to Live with a Ghost," will be released by Pearl City Press later this year.

5
A TASTE OF HOME

By Roxy Strike

When patrons step into Dog-Eared Books—Ames, Iowa's cozy independent bookstore—they enter a world of gleaming wooden shelves, comfortable reading nooks, and stories of love, loss, victory, and fantastical creatures. A place where imagination feels almost tangible. Few realize the darkness that lingers just beneath the floorboards.

The "Ber" months had always been Maricel Dhawan's favorite season. From September through December, Filipinos everywhere welcomed the world's longest Christmas celebration: carols sang in the humid air, *parol* lanterns glowing in icy windows, the promise of *lechon* and *bibingka* shared among friends. Even in Iowa, her mother kept the custom alive. Being half-Filipina and half-Pakistani never dulled Maricel's devotion to the "Ber" months.

This year, Maricel needed that joy more than ever.

She finally quit her job in Dallas, Texas, at one of the faceless financial companies where she had spent her twenties buried under spreadsheets and polite cruelty. The last cruelty was being passed over for a promotion she knew she had rightfully earned. Instead, the promotion went to Jordan, the newcomer she'd trained.

Maricel told herself that quitting was brave. She repeated it like a prayer while she packed up the framed certificates she never cared about and returned her laptop, which had been her entire world for far too many years. Brave, not reckless. Not giving up. Brave.

But as Maricel packed her apartment, sold her furniture, and sorted boxes full of desk plants and mismatched pens, she felt cracks in her prayer. She didn't feel brave. She felt like a balloon, slowly deflating, as she tried to figure out who she was.

Her mother, of course, had opinions.

"You're coming home," Pilar Dhawan said over the phone, voice clipped but steady. "Just for a little while. Until you decide what you're going to do next, *diba*?"

Her father, David, was more enthusiastic—well, as enthusiastic as a Pakistani reverend can be. "You can stay as long as you need. We'll get your old room ready."

And so, with a carful of clothes and books and the growing realization that she was 31 and moving back into her parents' house, Maricel started the long drive to Ames, Iowa.

***

Home. Was it still home? Maricel couldn't be sure. The Dhawan house hadn't changed. The white siding, the tree her father planted when she was seven, now a towering giant. The faded wooden manger her mother set up on the porch every year once the Ber months rolled around, complete with baby Jesus, stood in silent watch.

When Maricel stepped inside, she saw her mother's diminutive frame stirring a pot over the stove.

Pilar turned from the stove, hand on her hip, dish rag tossed over her shoulder. "Hello, *anak.*"

"Hey, Ma."

Pilar looked Maricel up and down, not unkindly, but a sharp assessment, nonetheless. "You look tired."

"Thanks, Ma," Maricel said, too worn out from the drive and disappointment of her lost career to fight.

Her father stepped into the kitchen and smiled. "Welcome home, beta."

The term of endearment should have warmed her, but instead, she felt empty.

***

Maricel didn't mean to get a job right away. But the silent looks from her mother and the idle time at home made her spiral. So, when she heard Dog-Eared Books was hiring, she jumped at the chance.

Avery, the owner of the cozy independent bookstore, was young and enthusiastic, flitting between rearranging displays and chatting with patrons about their latest reads.

"You worked in banking?" Avery asked Maricel, eyebrows raised. "So, you're not afraid of suffering. Perfect. You'll fit right in."

And like that, Maricel found herself working among the polished wood shelves, paper-wrapped books tied with twine, and the soft chatter of book lovers also searching for meaning between the pages and ink. The bookstore was everything her old corporate life wasn't: Slow. Warm. Human.

Maricel learned to make pour-over coffees. She learned how to ring up customers. She learned the names of each regular and that each had a personality that made every interaction unique.

Then, Avery announced to the staff they would be setting up a Christmas tree in the store and ready to light up on November 1st.

"We're going full Christmas spirit. Lean in, make it over the top," Avery instructed.

Maricel nodded; over-the-top Christmas was in her blood. She could do it. She had found her calling.

***

As a child, Maricel would join her father's church on crisp November evenings to decorate the sanctuary. Together, Maricel, her parents, and church members would gather in the Fellowship Hall to pull out boxes of dusty ornaments, garland, and the main attraction: the giant Christmas tree.

The tree always had a faint smell of pine from the scented pinecone ornaments packed into the box. One particular church member, Elaine, brought a tray of butter horns ready to share. Warm, buttery, and sugary sweet. Their scent always brought Maricel back to her first time meeting the kind old woman. It was comforting; it was home.

Elaine was ancient even then, with her silver hair, soft voice, and hands crisscrossed with veins. She'd welcomed the Dhawans when they first arrived from Texas, where people spoke Tagalog or Hindi in grocery aisles and nobody looked twice at their mixed-brown family. Moving to the rural state of Iowa scared Maricel, and—as an adult —she was sure the move scared her parents. In Iowa, kindness mattered more than likeness, and Elaine's kindness had saved them.

Maricel stayed with Elaine that first night while her parents unpacked from their move. As Elaine tucked Maricel in, brushing back her bangs, she whispered, "Let's say the Lord's Prayer together, shall we?" The touch of her papery hand and the scent of sugar from a day of baking butter horns made Maricel feel safe.

That first Christmas in Iowa was magical. It was the first real winter Maricel and her parents had experienced. Maricel's mother, who grew up in the tropical climate of the Philippines and only knew Texas winters (cold, rainy, rarely snowy), ran barefoot into the snow with Maricel. Maricel quickly realized she hated the cold after that. But Christmas, oh, Christmas was a different story.

Every Christmas Eve, Reverend Dhawan held a candlelight service. Maricel sat in the pew tucked in between her mother and Elaine. In the golden glow of candles and the soft singing of "Silent Night" by church members, Maricel felt the mystery and wonder of the holiday. Then, as she and her parents walked home to the parsonage, Maricel marveled at the clear night sky.

As their boots crunched across the snowy sidewalks, she looked for the legendary Star of Bethlehem to lead her home, just as it had guided the wise men to the manger. Maricel and her parents would stay up late making a parol —the paper star lantern without which no Filipino Christmas is complete —and eating butter horns that were never quite as good as Elaine's. Maricel felt warm and loved in those moments, knowing she had a community of friends and family in her father's church.

Now, decades later, the memories of Elaine and Christmas Eve lingered like candle smoke.

***

Avery dedicated the night of November 1st as Tree Night. The staff gathered in the store, with Mariah Carey's "Merry Christmas" album playing in the background. Avery wore a reindeer antler headband over her blond hair and handed out hot cocoa. The store was illuminated with soft light, and for one night, the world seemed at peace.

Then the bell over the front door chimed.

A blast of cold air swept in.

And Brody Anderson stepped inside.

Maricel's stomach flipped. Brody looked just like one of the lead male characters in a Hallmark Christmas movie—flannel shirt, snow-dusted curls, a smile that could brighten the room. He was the neighbor boy across the street, the one who helped her shovel the driveway and walked her home after school.

They drifted apart after high school. College. Jobs. Life. But now, there he was. With a box of used books on his hip.

"Hey, Avery, I have some books for the Christmas book drive," Brody called.

Avery waved him over while Maricel tried to busy herself with the ornament display, hoping Brody wouldn't see her. Too late.

"Mari?" Maricel turned, and Brody grinned like they were still 16. "Well, look who's back!"

She felt a pang of annoyance at the reminder that she was back home, living with her parents. But she couldn't stop smiling. "Hey, Brody."

"You got tired of being a titan of the banking industry," he joked.

"Oh yeah," Maricel deadpanned. "It was exhausting being so important and successful."

Brody laughed, a warm, rolling sound that made Maricel feel warm all over.

"You decorating the tree?" he asked.

Maricel nodded.

"Then I'm helping," he said.

Avery grinned, pretending not to notice.

The old friends hung ornaments side by side. Blown glass birds, felt animals, wooden snowflakes. Brody told her about taking over his family's bicycle shop. She shared stories about pivot tables and the exit interviews she'd cried through.

"You always belonged somewhere like this," he said, gesturing to the store.

The words hit too close. Maricel cleared her throat, irritated. "I'm not the girl I used to be, you know." Then, feeling guilty, Maricel added softly, "I don't know who I'm supposed to be anymore."

Brody didn't say anything, didn't try to fix it like Maricel's parents were always doing. He just stood with her. A warm, comforting presence.

***

The following days passed in a peaceful rhythm. Snowstorms blew through, and the town glittered in its winter coat of crystalline white. Dog-Eared Books became Maricel's sanctuary. The sound of children laughing, the crackle of heating vents, and the joy of patrons finding a new book or rediscovering stories from their youth. It felt like seeing color again after years of only grey.

Brody stopped by more often than could be explained with errands.

"You free later?" he asked one afternoon, leaning across the counter as Maricel restocked bookmarks.

Maricel shrugged. "Depends. Am I being kidnapped for hot cocoa or manual labor?"

"Both," Brody said cheerfully. "There's a Christmas market at the high school I thought we could check out, then you're helping me lift a thirty-pound wreath that I definitely cannot manage alone."

Maricel laughed. "Bold to assume I'm strong."

"Mari, I've seen you haul a stack of hardcover releases in one arm," he said. "You're unstoppable."

***

The Christmas market was filled with warm lights and laughter. High school students sold crocheted snowmen with crooked noses. Teens in red aprons ran the bake sale tables. And everyone seemed to know Brody, giving him high fives, thanking him for fixing their bikes, and for his family's donations to children in need.

He led her to a corner booth run by his family's store. Steaming gently, butter horns were fresh from the oven. Elaine's butter horns. Maricel's breath caught. "How did you find the recipe?" Maricel asked.

"My mom searched through old community recipe books until she found it," Brody said, suddenly shy. "I told her we should make them for your homecoming."

Maricel lifted the butter horn. The smell hit her first. Cinnamon and sugar and something faint beneath it, something like woodsmoke? Or something older.

She bit in.

Warmth flooded her.

But it was too warm, like a memory pressing against her from the inside. Her vision tunneled. The chatter of the market was muffled. The twinkling lights above flickered and held—too long—as though waiting for her to look back at them.

And just for a moment, someone whispered her name. So soft she couldn't tell if it was in her ear or her mind, *"Maricel."*

She blinked hard. The lights snapped back to normal. Brody was still there, smiling at her, oblivious.

She brushed a tear from her cheek before he could see it.

***

That night, dinner at the Dhawan house was quiet. Maricel barely touched her *dal makhani*, her favorite Punjabi dish made of black lentils and kidney beans seasoned with her father's secret garam masala blend.

"I saw you at the market. With Brody." Pilar's voice was gentle, but tight.

Maricel's shoulders stiffened. "Yes. We ran into each other."

"He's a good man," her mother said carefully. "Kind, rooted to the community."

The words lingered unspoken between them. *You were destined for more.*

Like many immigrants to the United States, Pilar was well-educated and worked as a teacher in the Philippines, but her credentials were not recognized in her new country. Pilar channeled her lost hopes and dreams into her daughter, leaving Maricel torn between fulfilling her family obligations and creating a life of her own. The ongoing struggle for a child of immigrants.

Seeing the tension between mother and daughter, her father, David, attempted to shift the conversation.

"We're decorating the church this week," he offered. "Maybe you'd like to help, beta? Like old times?"

Maricel wanted to say yes. She hadn't attended her father's church since returning home. She wanted to walk between the church pews again and breathe in the scent of evergreen and candlewax. But Pilar's silence pressed down.

Maricel picked up her spoon. "We'll see."

That night, Maricel lay awake in her childhood room, surrounded by posters of constellations and fictional worlds she once believed she could enter. She missed believing. She missed the wonder of Christmas. She missed feeling like joy wasn't something she had to chase or earn. The thought stayed in her chest, keeping her awake, and she wished she could live in her childhood memories of Christmas Eve.

As she tossed and turned, she noticed something on her bookshelf that she hadn't seen in years. Between the old *Chronicles of Narnia* paperbacks and high school yearbooks sat her father's battered Urdu folklore book. She suddenly remembered it—the one her father used to read when she couldn't sleep.

She pulled it from the shelf, the cover worn thin and the binding cracked. She flipped through the old pages until she found the illustration she remembered most: A woman smiling kindly, but the shadow behind her was wrong. Long arms, fingers like smoke, and eyes like burning charcoal.

It was the *djinn*. Or what her American classmates called a genie—a figure that for them conjured images of a blue, wisecracking cartoon. In the folklore of her father's homeland, the djinn was something more ambiguous and at times sinister. She looked at the image in the book. The shadow of the djinn seemed sharper. More defined. The fingers were even longer, curled, almost as if they were anticipating something.

Her father's voice echoed as she stared at the page, "Djinn do not come uninvited. Longing is a door we open ourselves."

Maricel slammed the book shut. Put it back and turned off the light. But the room smelled faintly of cinnamon. And when she closed her eyes, she felt something gently, almost lovingly, brush a strand of hair from her forehead.

Maricel swallowed a scream.

***

Two days later, snowfall blanketed the town. Brody found her shelving books in the romance section.

"Walk with me?" he asked.

They strolled down Main Street, past old brick storefronts, past the old train depot, past the church her father spent decades building into a community, one casserole and hymn at a time.

"You left because you needed space to grow," Brody said softly.

Maricel shoved her gloved hands deep into her coat pockets. She felt her defenses go up. "Maybe."

He looked at her with warmth in his eyes. "You don't have to go back to who you were in Dallas, Mari. And you don't have to recreate your childhood." His voice was calm, warm, grounded. "You just have to choose a life that feels right. A life that feels like you."

Something in her chest snapped.

"Yeah, well," she said, a little too sharp, "Some of us aren't meant to stay here forever. Some of us aren't meant to just..." She gestured toward the quiet street, the shops, and the church steepled against the sky. "Some of us aren't meant to settle."

Brody stopped walking. His expression wasn't angry. Just hurt. Deeply hurt.

"You think that's what this is? Settling?" he asked.

Maricel felt heat rising in her face, "Brody, I didn't mean…"

He cut her off. "No," he said steadily. "You said exactly what you meant."

The silence between them felt colder than the wind. Maricel blinked hard, trying to think of something to say to make things right again.

But, out of the corner of her eye, she thought she saw something. A single candle flickered in the church window, guttered, flared, and then died.

Brody didn't notice. Maricel did. A slow chill slid down her spine. Like someone had heard her longing. Like something had been waiting.

***

The next day, Maricel was in a daze. She had another sleepless night, longing for life to be simple again.

While Maricel slogged through work, Avery was light and cheerful. She played Christmas music loudly. Someone lit a sugar cookie-scented candle. The windows were fogged from the warmth inside the store and ice crystals sparkled against the glass.

Maricel hung a new ornament on the store tree, a felt star that reminded her of the parol she made as a child. And she let herself believe, just for a moment, that she could have both —past and present, love and memories —steady in where she'd been, and running to what could be.

She caught a faint scent of cinnamon. Not the warm cozy scent from the candle, but something dry and distant. Like a memory from childhood, she could almost place it but not quite reach it.

She turned and saw Brody. He caught Maricel's eye and lifted two steaming to-go cups of hot cocoa from the café down the street. He crossed the floor, his chiseled face pink from the cold, snowflakes melting in his curls.

"Truce?" he asked, offering Maricel one. "If you promise not to laugh at how many marshmallows I asked for in them."

She took the drink, feeling her hands and heart warm instantly. "Thanks, Brody. I...."

He shook his head and stopped Maricel. "I'm just glad you're home, Mari. Even if it's just for now."

Maricel and Brody stood together next to the tree, glowing with lights and jingling with ornaments. Maricel opened her mouth, maybe to answer him, or perhaps to admit something she wouldn't let herself believe yet.

A cold wind slid under the door. The lights flickered. Then the bell above the door chimed. An old woman stepped inside.

***

"Hello, can I help you find anything?" Maricel asked, glancing away from Brody before she froze.

The woman looked exactly like Elaine. Same small frame, same curls of white hair, same watery blue eyes that seemed to see through her. The woman smiled, the same knowing smile Maricel remembered from childhood.

Maricel almost called her Elaine, but Elaine passed away years ago.

"Yes," the woman said in a gravelly voice. "Avery has a package for me."

"I'll grab her for you," Maricel said, forcing brightness into her voice. She checked the back office, empty. When she returned, the store had gone strangely quiet.

"Avery must've stepped out," she said. "Can I take your name, and I'll let her know you stopped by?"

"Oh, that's quite all right," the woman murmured. "It's downstairs, in the storage room."

The staff jokingly called the storage room The Crypt—a dirt-floored room in the basement. It smelled of paper, dust, and the faint metallic tang of rusting pipes. A world apart from the warm space above.

The old woman smiled again, but the smile didn't quite reach her eyes. "It's just down the stairs, beta. I'm sure it can't be too hard to find."

The term of endearment gave Maricel cold dread rather than comfort, but customer service was ingrained in Maricel, whether she was working in an office or in a cozy bookstore in a quaint town. "I...Yes, absolutely, ma'am. I'll be right back," Maricel said.

"Why don't I come by the bike shop after I finish up here this evening," Maricel whispered to Brody as she walked past. "We'll make parol together, yeah?"

"Can't wait," Brody said as he smiled.

***

Maricel hesitated as she approached the door to the basement. Why was she so afraid to go downstairs and grab a small package for an old woman who looked and, Maricel suddenly realized, smelled like Elaine. She turned to glance at the woman, who had not moved from the Christmas tree with that not-quite-a-smile on her face. Maricel shuddered, flicked the light switch, and descended the stairs.

Each step down felt heavier than the last. Maricel thought about running back upstairs to wait for Avery, but she scolded herself. She'd dealt with giants of the banking industry. She could deal with an unsettling old woman who looked like her surrogate grandma. She steeled her nerves and continued to the basement, each step creaking, and beneath it, the faintest hint of cinnamon. "Jesus, am I having a stroke?" Maricel joked to herself.

Maricel reached the bottom of the stairs and turned to face the warped door of The Crypt. She grasped the doorknob and slowly opened it. The movement caused chipped white paint to flake across the dirt floor, like the snow whirling outside. She pulled the string for the light in The Crypt. The single bulb hummed on but emitted little more than a wavering yellow glow.

Boxes lined the walls of The Crypt like silent sentinels, waiting. Something faintly glimmered in the corner. Maricel crossed the dirt-packed floor and found a parcel wrapped in something familiar. She gasped. It was wrapped in the tissue paper she used as a child to make parol, and old church bulletins. As Maricel's fingertips brushed the parcel, the air shifted and exhaled.

The light sputtered out, then flared white-hot. The basement floor tilted under her feet, no longer cool dirt, but warm, polished wood. The scent of dust turned to pine and sugar. When Maricel gathered her senses, she looked up and realized she was no longer in The Crypt.

Snow blew against the towering stained-glass windows, and the church sanctuary glowed with warm candlelight and indistinct chatter. Her father laughed as he hung garland on the pulpit rail while her mother's trained soprano sang out *Silent Night.* And there, by the tree, stood Elaine. Smiling, whole, *alive,* as if twenty years had never passed since their last time together.

"Elaine?" Maricel breathed out. Her throat tightened. Just like when the old woman upstairs called her "beta," Maricel felt dread rather than comfort. "How? How are you here?"

"Beta," Elaine said, her voice low and smooth as smoke curling from a fire. "You're home. You asked me to return. I am only answering."

Tears stung Maricel's eyes as she gulped several times, trying to grasp where and *when* she was. "I don't understand," she barely managed to whisper. "I didn't ask for you. I only wanted to remember."

"You asked for meaning, beta," Elaine said. "For joy again. I can give it to you. You need only stay here, in this time. In this place."

Maricel squeezed her eyes shut, forcing down the panic rising in her chest. She slowly opened them, and the bright Christmas colors around her pulsed too bright, too sharp. The candles melted upward. Her father's laughter looped maniacally, and her mother's song repeated the same lyric in increasing crescendo, over and over again, for what felt like eternity. "Jesus. Lord at Thy birth. JESUS. Lord at Thy Birth. JESUS. LORD AT THY BIRTH."

Elaine's face distorted into a swirling, menacing nothingness. Behind her, the ornaments made of glittering felt put there year after year for decades turned to look at Maricel.

"I don't think this is real," Maricel's voice trembled. "I think... I think...."

A deep, glaring crack began to appear across the roiling mass of Elaine's face, a grotesque smile.

"You misunderstand, beta. You were happier then. I can return you to that," the thing said. Its voice echoed with a thousand memories. "Why leave? Why change? Here, your joy is preserved. Forever."

As the smile cracked the nothingness, the scent of cinnamon thickened, cloying, until it consumed the air around Maricel.

Maricel gagged. "No...no, this isn't real."

"Oh, but it is," the thing whispered, right beside her ear, even though it had not moved. "Longing is the most real thing you have known."

The candles winked out, one by one, and a single word slammed into Maricel's mind: *djinn.* How could Maricel forget her father's family stories? Djinn, the ancient creatures who lived in the empty spaces of every wish. Whose very smiles promised salvation but left ruin. It was a djinn, not Elaine, who feasted on her Christmas wish, and it was a djinn that bound Maricel to the velvety darkness as she screamed out.

***

The light slowly flickered back on. Maricel stood once again on the dirt floor of The Crypt, alone and clinging desperately to the package. Dust drifted through the air as the smell of cinnamon wafted around her. Maricel, frozen in terror, looked through the door of The Crypt and saw a single beam of light from the top of the stairs. "Hello?" Maricel called. Her voice felt muted by the walls of the basement, leaving her feeling even smaller than her five-foot-two frame and infinitely more frightened than she had in her life. She heard no reply.

Her terror broken by the emptiness, she ran to the stairs and climbed them two at a time, reaching out her hand for the door to reality, to warmth. The door didn't budge. Maricel rammed her shoulder against the door again and again. As she fought back sobs, she heard the muffled sounds of life on the other side. The gentle murmur of conversation, a child crying, the ring of the register.

"Avery!" Maricel screamed. "Please! Stop whatever this is! Brody, please, I'm down here!"

No one heard. The sounds above went on. Paper bags rustled. Children giggled. Someone asked for gift wrap. Mariah Carey's "All I Want for Christmas Is You" floated through the speakers. Maricel slumped, breathless, to the top step as the package slipped through her fingers. It landed with a dull thud.

The twine slowly unraveled, along with the red, gold, green, and blue tissue paper, as the cracking old bulletins folded back like petals. Inside, Maricel thought she saw a hint of green and red felt, trimmed in gold glitter. It was a star, similar to those the old church ladies used to make. At its center was a glowing ember.

"Elaine?" Maricel whispered as she pressed her forehead against the wooden door. Her voice cracked as she spoke, a whisper, not for anyone but herself. "I just wanted to go back home. I just wanted the Christmas I remember, before life got in the way."

Maricel's throat tightened. "But home isn't a memory. I should have made a new Christmas, with what I have now." And she cried as she resumed pounding at the door. "Please, let me go back. I know now. I know. I know...."

Then, a breath, warm and sweet as cinnamon, brushed past her ear. "Let's say the Lord's Prayer together, shall we?"

***

Brody didn't notice at first. Not the shift. Not the absence.

Just a feeling, like stepping into a room where someone had been a moment ago, and the air was still warm with their presence.

He was halfway down Main Street when the sensation sharpened. A thrum in his chest, faint and hollow. Something—or was it someone—was missing.

He stopped walking. Looked back. The street was the same as it always was, snow piled in the gutters, holiday lights blinking softly, shop windows glowing against the darkening winter sky.

But something in him told him to go back. Back to the bookstore. He turned and he ran.

The bell chimed overhead as he pushed inside Dog-Eared Books. Warmth and laughter washed over his cold face. Avery chatted at the counter. A child begged for a sticker. Someone hummed along to the Christmas playlist.

Normal, perfectly normal.

Brody's gaze flicked through the store, searching for a face he couldn't picture, a voice he couldn't quite remember. A presence he felt more than he knew. His breath quickened.

"Hey, are you okay?" Avery asked.

He swallowed. "Have you seen…"

The name dissolved the moment he reached for it. He tried again.

"I think… I was meeting someone here."

Avery's brow softened with concern. "You came in earlier to drop off those donated books, remember? Maybe you're just tired from the holiday retail season."

Brody nodded, but everything felt off. Like his movements didn't match something deep down he knew was wrong.

He wandered through the store, past the counter and tables of bestsellers. He felt drawn to the Christmas tree. Something was missing from the branches. He lifted his hand, fingers hovering over that empty spot among the lights and ribbon and glitter.

A felt star, maybe? Red and green. Glitter around the edges.

His chest tightened. His eyes burned. For no reason, his throat closed around a sudden, sharp grief. So sharp he nearly choked.

Avery noticed him. "Brody, what's wrong?"

He wiped his eyes. "I don't know." And he didn't know. He only knew that he stood *right here*, next to someone whose laugh he should remember. Whose warmth he should feel. Someone who fit beside him like a second heartbeat.

But the memory floated away. It was gone, like a shape left in the snow, slowly melting and smoothing into white.

***

Dog-Eared Books hummed with the cheerful noise of the holiday shopping season. Pages turned as patrons looked for the perfect gift, steaming mugs of coffee warmed cold hands, and someone laughed a little too loudly at a joke. Life continued on. Bright. Ordinary.

Brody stepped back from the tree, taking shallow breaths. Outside, the town glittered in the winter night. Inside, the scent of cinnamon wafted through the floorboards. And below, in the locked and silent dark, someone banged once on a wooden door. No one ever heard.

***

About the Author

Roxy Strike believes stories connect our communities. She'll happily regale anyone with tales about her pets, new hair colors, crafting, and the ghost child who lives in her house. You can usually find Roxy and her husband thrifting around Ames and spending too much money on coffee.

6

'TWAS A RELATIVELY MINOR NIGHT BEFORE CHRISTMAS

By Vicki Minor

Twas the night before Christmas,

when all through the house

Not a creature was stirring ... that

snoring was my spouse!!

The stockings were *not* hung by

the chimney with care—

They were still in the dryer ...
WHO LEFT THEM THERE!?

One dog was nestled all snug in
my bed,
The other in a kennel on her
back, legs outspread.
Buried under numerous blankets, due to the winter crap,
We all bedded down for a
well-deserved nap.

When out on the lawn there
arose such a clatter,
I yelled at the dogs, "Quit barking," there's nothing the matter.

The full moon above with its vibrant white glow
Cast a bright light on trees and
snow down below.
When what to my wondering
eyes should appear,
Yup, it was Santa's sleigh and
those darn reindeer.

Santa, his suit all red velvet with
white,
Called out reindeer names, eight
of them that night.
He said their names loud so they
would understand,
Listen, I am Santa! This Christmas, I'm the man!

Now, Dasher! Now, Dancer!
Now, Prancer and Vixen!
(Hmm, Vixen ... that must be a
female reindeer?)
On, Comet! On, Cupid! On,
Donner and Blitzen!

Santa steadily guided the sleigh
towards the roof.
The reindeer set down, first right
then left hoof.
One reindeer lost his balance,
but, was able to right—
Wouldn't be good to drop a
sleigh of toys at midnight

As I stood there in awe of what
was abound,
I realized we had no chimney for
Santa to come down.
I thought for a moment, then a
moment more,
I would just motion him over to
the front door.

I opened the door laughing, in
spite of myself,
In front of me stood Santa, the
jolly old elf.
I apologized for the inconve-
nience: no fireplace to come
down.
He said, "No problem!" as he put
his sack on the ground.

Santa didn't speak much as he
went to work,
I told him the stockings were still
in the dryer. (I felt like a jerk.)
He paused for a moment, then
looked straight at me.

Santa had noticed we didn't have
a tree!

He said, "Listen to me tonight,
young miss, and take heed,
Christmas isn't about all the stuff
you get,
It's about sharing, caring, and
acts of good deed."

As he sprang to his sleigh on the
eve of the 25th,
He said, "This year, friends and
family
Will be your most treasured gift!
Merry Christmas to all, and to all
have a great night!"

***

About the Author

Vicki Minor serves as editor of the Winterset Madisonian, where she not only reports on the pulse of the community but also flexes her funny bone in a weekly column. Her writing extends beyond the newsroom to Substack, where she publishes her newsletter *Relatively Minor*—a playful nod to her belief that laughter doesn't need a major source. It can be, well, relatively minor. On the same platform, she also curates *Narratives and Notes*, a thoughtful series exploring the creative practices of writers and songwriters from Iowa and beyond.

7

AN ORDINARY WINTER DAY

BY MICHAEL KAUFMAN

Overnight, the wind blew the falling snow into drifts all around the house and outbuildings of the farm. The snow reflected the fresh light of the sun which had just crested the white plains. The wind still blew, and occasionally a clump of powdery snow would be carried away. Cattle were in the lot huddling around the full hay rings near the fence where the calving shed took the brunt of the wind.

Tom Raleigh stepped out of his house feeling the cold air on his cheeks and nose. His lip carried a fresh dip of tobacco, and his gloved hand carried a thermos full of black coffee. The wind took his breath as he passed the garage into the open yard. His eldest son, Phil, who was eight, wide eyed and smiling, followed close behind as they trudged through the snow-covered yard. Phil hoped whatever they were doing would be quick so he could go back inside and open presents. The fresh, cold air and snow took his mind from such thoughts.

"Look at all the bird tracks," said Phil. "And there's Mollie's tracks," he said pointing at the paw prints in the snow.

"Yep," said Tom.

"Where did she go?"

"She's probably playing or chasing squirrels and rabbits in those trees."

"I should go help her with my BB gun."

"I thought you were helping me," said Tom.

"Oh. I am. What are we doing? I thought we gave the cows plenty of hay yesterday before the snow."

"We did. We're going to check them to see if they had any calves in this weather."

"I thought we calve in January and February."

"We do, but I turned the bull out a little early this year. And when the vet preg-checked these cows there were a few due in early January. And I noticed a couple were close."

"How could you tell?"

"Some things are swollen."

"Swollen?" said Phil. "What things?"

Tom did not answer but climbed the gate to the lot and was over with a swing of his leg. Phil stepped on each rung smiling to the top where he sat, legs dangling, looking at the cows who were looking at him.

"I don't see any babies," said Phil.

"You've got to look harder. They could be anywhere. It's almost never the obvious or most convenient spot."

Tom traversed the snowy, high mound of the lot over to the herd. Phil stayed atop the gate keeping his chin in his coat. Tom walked among the herd counting and looking for any signs of birth.

"We're missing one," said Tom as he spit into the snow leaving a brown spot. "I counted twice and got the same thing."

Phil, from the gate, pointed at each cow trying to count them. "How many should there be?" he asked.

"Forty-seven," said Tom. "I knew I should have shut them in the lot last night," he said quietly to himself.

"I keep losing count," said Phil.

"We're missing one," said Tom. "Go open the driveway gate into the pasture and wait for me."

Tom got the side-by-side from the shop and picked up Phil, waiting curiously by the open gate.

"What are we doing?" asked Phil.

Tom swallowed a mouthful of hot coffee. "Going to find the missing cow," he said.

"What if we can't find her?"

"She's out here somewhere. We just have to look. A black cow in white snow can't stay hidden for long."

"What if she has a calf?"

"She more than likely does being out here alone. I should have had the gate shut to the pasture last night. Damn foolish mistake."

Tom drove over the hill, keeping in the shallower snow away from the drifts. The hilly plains were white layers all the way to the horizon. The barbed wire fences were lines in the snow with random trees in the rows, having been seeds dispersed from birds resting atop the posts.

"Come spring we need to get the chainsaw and cut those little trees there in that fence before their grown and entangled in it," said Tom.

"What about all those big ones by the pond down there?" asked Phil.

"No. Those make good shade for the cows in the summer."

Down the hill around the dam of the pond near the fence stood the missing cow. She was alert and shifting her head and eyes back and forth between the approaching side-by-side and a small black object nearly under the fence. Afterbirth hung in front of her tail.

"Sure enough," said Tom. He parked close to the calf keeping the cow on the other side.

"Is it alive?" asked Phil leaning over the seat.

"Looks like it. But barely in this wind. You stay in here. That cow won't be friendly."

Tom went out to inspect the calf leaving the door open. The wind and snow whirled around the cab. Phil looked out the window at the nervous cow, keeping her eyes on his dad. She paced back and forth, the condensation showing with each breath she took. Then she walked around the front of the side-by-side and let out a bellow which was masked by the cold air. Phil was on his knees on the seat leaning against the dash. Tom picked the calf up and laid it on the floor. It lay there in a heap, its nose and ears down. Tom closed the door, turned the floor heat to high and drove off. Phil watched the cow out the back window. She sniffed where the calf had laid then looked up and bellowed again.

"What about the cow?" asked Phil.

"She might follow," said Tom. "Or we'll get her later."

Phil suddenly remembered the calf was on the floor. He sat down and touched it with his bare hands, cold and wet. He felt sorry for it. Though he smiled at the thought of it riding with them. "Is it a boy or girl?" he asked.

"It's a little bull."

"Well, we found him. And saved him."

"Not yet we haven't."

"Won't he be okay now?"

"I'll believe it when I see it," said Tom.

They followed the tracks they made before. A few times Tom stopped, rolled the window down, and made a sound like a calf until the cow would follow again at a trot. Phil noticed after finding the calf the excitement had dwindled some. There was a sense it was not all that he expected or all he thought it would be. The calf lay there near death, in a pile, and seemed lesser than Phil had imagined. It was so meek and helpless. He tried to make sense of it the best he could. Tom might have felt that way too once, or thought more about it, but he had seen it enough and grown used to it. He was focused now on ensuring the calf would survive and would be satisfied only when he witnessed its survival.

The cattle in the lot had not moved. All of nature was waiting out the wind. The inside of the cab was hot and dry. The only part of the calf that moved was its side with each slow breath it took. Phil kept putting his hand between its rib and stomach where its flat hair would rise and fall. He hoped the calf would survive. He wanted to believe the calf would survive. So, he believed. He had not the experience for disbelief. He had never thought much about purpose but now he was. He wondered why the calf had been born on such a cold morning and why his mother had borne him in such a spot. Why would it come only to die so soon? Besides that, within a year or two the calf would be killed for food.

"I was thinking," said Phil. "We try to keep the calf alive just to kill it later."

"That's one way we make money," said Tom. "And everyone needs to eat."

"Seems funny is all."

"Sometimes it takes dying to see the reason for living."

"I just hope he survives for now," said Phil.

Tom thought of what to do next and how to keep the calf alive. He had no time for hope. He noticed the mother had followed them into the lot.

"When we stop you go around and shut the gate to the pasture," said Tom. "Stay out of the lot. Then come back and I'll be in the calving shed."

***

When Phil closed the door to the shed and felt the wind cease, his dad was in the corner by the shelves and equipment opening the calf's mouth and holding its head up with one big arm wrapped around it and the other holding a bottle and tube.

"What are you doing now?" asked Phil.

"Tubing this calf."

"What's that stuff again?"

"Colostrum. It's like milk. Gives him nutrients and energy."

"Doesn't his momma give him milk?"

"Hopefully she will. She hadn't yet. Her tits hadn't been touched."

"How do you know?"

"They weren't shiny or clean. He's had no milk. All she did was lick him clean from birth. Take that towel and dry him."

"Like this?" asked Phil.

"Yep."

"He's done with the milk stuff?"

"Yep. I must have got the right hole too."

"What do you mean?"

"It went to his belly and not his lungs."

"What if it went to his lungs?"

"He'd be dead. Now open that calf warmer."

Phil opened the lid on the warmer that looked like a doghouse and Tom laid the calf in it. The calf, for the first time, lifted its head with its own power. Tom closed the lid and turned on the warmer.

"Now what?" asked Phil.

"We wait."

"How long?"

"Quite a while."

***

Once they pinned the cow in the shed, she paced and sniffed the dirt and straw. Phil ran to the house to tell his mom and brothers about the calf, eager to spread the news. Above Tom's whiskery cheeks his skin was red. He squinted his eyes in the light beaming off the snow. The automatic water in the lot had frozen. The wind nipped at his wet, bare hands as he worked to adjust the float which had been stuck in the ice. The cattle heard the rushing water and circled around him ready to drink.

Tom cursed aloud his troubles though he knew them so well. They were nothing new. To manage without them would be unrealistic. To wish them away would be foolish. They were part of life as much as anything was. To believe the calf would live, would be to forget the ones who had not lived. But something genuine and joyful remained inside Tom, ready to be released if it did survive. If it proved itself. And he knew what day it was. He knew his family was inside in the warmth safe and sound. Through all the troubles there was plenty of good to hang on to. It could always be worse. He cursed his troubles anyway.

***

The heat of the house stung Tom's hands and cheeks. His eyes adjusted to the duller, artificial light. The tree was lit in the living room. The smell of coffee and breakfast filled the house. Tom picked up a toddler who ran to him chewing on a piece of bacon. Jade, Tom's wife, looked tired holding a baby. She smiled and gave Tom a kiss on the cheek.

"Your cheeks are freezing," said Jade.

"Damn wind is cold," said Tom.

"Philip told us all about the new calf."

"He was pretty excited out there."

"Do you think the calf will make it?"

"We'll see."

"I bet he will," she said. "You know what you're doing."

"If I'd known what I was doing the cow would have been pinned in that shed last night."

Phil came running into the dining room. "Did you get the water working?" he asked.

"Yep," said Tom. "You need to eat some breakfast."

Tom sat the toddler in a highchair and the three of them ate eggs, bacon, and toast.

The cold wind could be heard like aches inside the house. At the table, only Tom noticed. It was a reminder that the harsh reality of life was still there. Nothing manmade could change that. It only stifled the truth. There would always be coming and going, living and dying, loss of faith and finding faith in whatever or whomever it may be in. It was rarely clear. Faith would forever be tried. Hope and love too. Nothing was certain. It was there to take it or leave it.

The day was like any other day for Tom. It was that way for Jade too, but she was better at believing. She did not need to see every detail happen before trusting in it.

"Do you want to open your presents now?" asked Jade.

"No," said Phil. "I want to make sure the calf is okay before I open any. If that's okay."

"Sure it is," said Jade. "There are more important things."

"When will we go back out, dad?" asked Phil.

"We've still got time."

Soon the house was filled with the smell of baking cookies. Tom felt the warmth getting to his fingers and face, but it would take a wash in a hot shower to beat the chill in his bones. The baby sat in his bouncer. The other two boys played on the living room floor. Jade cuddled on Tom's lap in the easy chair. It was cozy and peaceful. Something Tom truly believed in because it was there in front of him. He could feel it and touch it and see it. There was no mystery or need for interpretation. It was.

***

Outside the wind gusted. Phil played in the snow with the dog, Mollie. They both ran to catch up with Tom.

"What will happen if the calf doesn't drink from his momma?" asked Phil.

"We would try to bottle feed it."

"And if that doesn't work?"

"Then it dies," said Tom.

Mollie began barking at something way off by the creek that ran straight along the bottom ground through the snow-covered fields. She took off after it, barking, her collie coat flowing in the wind.

"What does she see?" asked Phil.

"Who knows," said Tom. "A tree or a deer. Maybe a coyote. She likes showing us she's guarding the place."

"That's all she knows, isn't it?"

"That's right. It's a simple doctrine she lives by. Everything is what it is for her."

Inside the shed was calm and quiet. The cow was alert to their presence. Tom shut her in the headgate with the side panel removed so that her legs and underside were exposed. He got the calf out of the warmer. It was lively. He helped it along to the cow's head so she could smell it. The calf let out the deepest call it could manage with its mouth wide open and tongue straight out. The cow sniffed the calf all over then jerked her head around slinging saliva and rattling the metal of the headgate. Tom walked the calf to the cow's hind quarters. Then nudged it toward her udder. The calf wobbled then stood. It veered one way then another then found the udder with its nose then scooped up a teat with its tongue and began to suck.

Tom smiled closed mouth. Phil grinned wide showing teeth.

"My God," said Tom. "I guess he'll make it."

"He was pretty much dead," said Phil. "Now look at him. Alive. Beats any presents I'll get."

"It is a good feeling isn't it."

After tending to the cow and calf, Tom and Phil walked back to the house. Tom thought about needing to plow the driveway. Phil wondered why the excitement had left again so soon. Purpose and meaning crept into his mind like the cold wind.

***

About the Author

Michael Kaufman is a Navy veteran working in the construction field. While in the military, he began writing as a hobby. After being discharged, he obtained a bachelor's degree in history and is currently working on an MFA in creative writing. He resides where he grew up, in rural, southwest Iowa with his beautiful wife and four wonderful boys.

8

PEARS IN THE PINE TREE

By Katrina Sogaard Anderson

There was once a decade in which a half mile of luminaries showed up in Beaufort, Iowa on Christmas Eve. They seemed to appear out of nowhere, sandwich sack angels lighting the way toward the north Dubuque County crossroad at dusk. Every three feet, a paper sandwich bag weighted by a scoop of sand hosting the live flame of a votive candle.

This miracle must have been performed while the town was preparing the dinner for after Mass, wrapping presents, or getting themselves ready for church. There was a small list of suspected luminarians. It included the mayor, the church secretary, the school janitor, the group of six elementary teachers (two of whom were nuns), and even the undertaker, though he was a long shot, living over in Buena Vista.

The illumination was explained to the young ones as the possible work of the wood elves from White Pine Hollow as a reward to the well-behaved children. Some suspected it to be a gift from the old hermit who lived deep down a winding gravel lane on a bluff overlooking the

Mississippi, extending his arms to the community for the first time in recent memory.

But no one owned up to it. The design and implementation of the four lighted corners was a well-kept secret in a town that was normally terrible at keeping them. The geometric precision of more than eight hundred luminaries had the respect of everyone—the children from the sizable farm families and the town kids alike; the influential night-hawk Cleve, who kept bar at the Four Way; Mr. Nicholas Andre, father of six and keeper of the Andre General Store; the group of stoic farmers that met for coffee at the Feed & Seed every Monday. Both the morning banker and the late-day banker had their own theories, based mainly on who had taken larger withdrawals than usual recently.

During early-winter years, the candled sacks were stacked on snow-banks, safely ensconced by the ice and glowing even more brilliantly as they reflected off the prismatic frozen water vapor. In more mild years they were placed on the mostly maintained cobblestones of the roadway.

These bedrocks lined the curb edge in front of the cornerstones of Beaufort. Woven together, the four bastions of commerce and community: the gas station, the tavern, the Andre General Store, and the steepled heights of Holy Trinity Catholic Church. The church was bricked with the same hues of orange, purple, and dark red that lined the rough intersection and walled the neighboring school. The town was anchored by the church. And the church, having been paid for by a collective of sixty families and built by the skilled laborers of their locality in 1875, was the pride of the town.

By the third year of the luminaries, other magic sprung up; in a particular yard, coniferous trees fruited, somehow producing perfectly ripened treasures. Homemade caramels, small gemstones, and hand-carved reindeer started showing up in mailboxes. Green, fragrant boughs anonymously arched over the school entry for the last week before break.

The lighted years for Juliana Rose Andre were ages seven to seventeen. Daughter of the third-generation general store-keep Nic and his wife, Bertha, Julie's early wonder and surprise matured to appreciation of the project's humility and curiosity about its orchestration each Christmas. Her five younger siblings had their own experiences with the decade of light—it fell differently on their timelines and meant other things to them. But as the oldest child, when she finally got a sense of the power of that role, Julie played up the mythology and the mystery. Before bed, all December, she'd remind the littler ones to look for signs of the elves tomorrow.

When Julie made the trip northeast for Christmas break after her first semester at state college, she anticipated the warm embrace of home, her parents' store and well-stocked pantry. Her brothers were eager for stories and the treats she had written about. Her sisters were desperate to have their hair braided properly, since Julie's plaiting skills surpassed those of their mother.

She rode home with a carpool of other area collegiates, thinking of the bright mile. It gave her the feeling of being a kid again after a long semester of trying on adulthood, being on her own, and finding other kinds of magic down in Iowa City.

Upon her return, her mom needed her help in the kitchen. Julie happily donned her old apron when it was handed to her, dusting off her sous-chef skills. With the meal ready and staying warm in the low oven, and all eight Andres dressed in their finest, her sister June brought her a matching sprig of pine with hot-glued red berries to pin in her hair as everyone put on their coats.

But as the Andres set out for the Christmastide service, it was to a bleak, unlit landscape. The streetlights were reflecting off the earlier rain that had frozen slightly on the road and walks, but the street was otherwise dark.

Following her family up the hill felt colder than it should have despite the mild temperature that night and the chirping excitement of the younger kids that resiliently moved on in anticipation of stockings and pie. Dad patted the railing as they walked past their store, tucked in for the night and following day. Julie asked her mother what she thought had happened. Bertha looked in the distance past the town, over hills and into the horizon, and absolved, "Well, they didn't get them out in time."

The missing luminaries sat heavy with Julie—it felt like an end to something. For the entirety of the Christmas Eve Liturgy, she heard the familiar songs but found herself humming the tune instead of gleefully caroling the words as she pondered the shadows in the corners of the church. The flower arrangements at the altar, were they smaller this year? Her parents and the other parishioners were participating as normal, if a little downcast. The adults had known many Christmas Eves before the lights yet had grown accustomed to the glow like everyone else.

Julie had questions. Had the luminarian fallen ill, or perhaps the mystery lamplighter had died while she was away? Had she somehow broken the spell by leaving? What other earthly magic was conditional? What else might disappear one day?

***

Juliana Rose Andre Fredricksen set her newly inherited table with duty and delight. It wouldn't be the whole family around the table, but it would be a plenty big group. One, two... three, four... five at the kids' table: they'd agreed to put her sister's clever but noisy kids in their own adjacent room with plenty of sound absorption. Two, four... six, eight... twelve at the big table. She and Drake would host her two sisters and all three of their families for what they were this year calling the Winter Solstice Gathering.

Julie touched each of the various chairs, tucking the patchwork set neatly into place. The lone child still under their roof, Otto, had been helping her gather them this week: his bedroom desk chair, her office chair, the sewing chair (could it still be called that if no one in the house sewed anymore?), the four from the basement game table. She knew they'd be fighting over who got to sit on the cushy orange folded set from the closet, relics from their parents' Friday night card parties.

Otto had pulled chairs that she didn't even know were still there; another way that this year felt like rediscovery of a faraway land, her family's recent takeover of her childhood home sinking in as time passed. Each item pulled from a back room or deep cupboard produced bouts of nostalgia and what might be called grief.

A walk to the shuttered church was not on the agenda this year, but then, it hadn't been for Julie for a few years now. These days, the parish church was staffed and opened for only scheduled weddings and funerals. Her mother's generation flocked dutifully, on foot, to Mass twice weekly. That was a thing of the past; the modern masses drove forty minutes to the old Wal-Mart turned megachurch in Dubuque on Sundays.

Outside the early afternoon windows, the wind blew tossed in several directions, each gust a suggestion of snow. Julie thought back to a PBS show that her mother often played in the background when she was a child. She would get super close to the little TV in the kitchen to immerse herself in the painting instruction. The old-fashioned looking painter might describe her yard right now in his soft, lulling baritone, "Just a *hint* of snow starting to gather on the brown lawn. A little speckle of white blowing in. And over here, we'll tuck a small bench next to this house, inviting us to sit down. Won't you sit for a moment, take a short break in your day? Now, a swipe of vermillion from your palette with your two-inch brush, we're going to throw the *idea* of a hill rising up from that happy brick cottage. There's no perfection, just your imagination. That's right, throw that hill behind the house, a dance with your brush. Just a flick. You could sled down it if you wanted. Many have before. There's a whole winter party getting started in that house.

You can't see it, but you can feel it, can't you? Feel the warmth of their oven just *glowing* out of the windows. A yellow ochre mist with your blender brush, just a touch of cad yellow."

Her eyes traveled along, a #2 liner brush on the windowpane, and stopped at the happy little grove of white pines edging the neighbor's yard. The trees stood as a coven, holding branch hands in a circle. Her sisters were coming! She remembered how they sat in those trees as kids: the low, sturdy branches gave them a second home in every season. Their brothers used them as target practice for their bows and arrows or bb guns. The sisters would chase them off, "Find a target that isn't a living being!" Julie remembered Deannie shouting once.

Her sisters: June Patricia Andre and Deandra Sharon Andre. Each had found alternative avenues to spirituality in their post-Christian adulthood, one that was closer at hand in nature and easier found in meditation and energetic healing than it was reciting choral monotone prayers indoors in a pack.

However, their three brothers had decided or been convinced by their wives to attend church at the Wal-Mart after the diocese stopped paying a priest and locked the Holy Trinity doors. Theirs were a few of the oversized pickup trucks that necessitated two DPD officers to direct traffic on Highway 20 each Sunday. When Alan decided that this was the year to travel for an all-inclusive tropical vacation at Christmas, both Jerry and Dave jumped at the chance and their wives cheered not having to cook. The sisters convened and saw it as a chance to gather on their more aligned terms.

For their first holidays ever, they could cling to their old plans or throw them to the wind. It seemed everyone was comfortable with the latter. The power of this experiment for the sisters, since they would be gathering in the same place as always, hinged on the renaming of the event as it approached, and making a few non-negotiable changes: an outdoor bonfire in addition to the basement bar cocktail ritual and the single, name-drawn gift exchange that would be a central fixture of their time after dinner instead of the two-hour, Santa-hat gift extravaganza.

For decades, they had all left with Mom's Christmas with armfuls of presents, an overgenerous amount. Were the piles of gifts obligatory and bereft of meaning, or was each little mass-produced item full of intention? Though it seemed the recipients had been thoughtfully considered, what happened to a personalized beanbag when its owner died? How useful was a personal foot bath? The microplastics contained in a single Bed Bath & Beyond were nightmare-inducing.

The sisters would try a new way of gifting, something that would address the agreed-upon cardinal sin of materialism. Deannie thought there should be a requirement to make a gift from scratch, but not everyone was as crafty as Deannie. June thought everyone should write a poem and print copies to hand out, but that was pretty specific. They settled on Julie's idea of a name-draw with a suggested spending amount and encouraged everyone to do their research on their recipient's list of wants.

Julie called to her husband in the next room, "Drake, love, do you think that June and Deannie will want to sit next to their husbands? I mean, partners? You know what I mean." Preferred descriptors were a work in progress for this near elder. She thought that seating the sisters together might turn them into an impenetrable clique, as could be their tendency.

"Hm – what? Are you setting places? Should we be making name cards?" His sleepy voice gave away how deep he had been in his grading work.

"I guess I'm just thinking about where I might put them, if people expect me to... orchestrate things like Mom used to?"

He peeked his head around the corner from his desk, his chair, not yet available to move to the table, as he was finishing feedback on his students' sustainable land use proposals before the break. "Don't you think everyone can handle choosing their own seat, Jewel?"

"Well. Maybe." Julie furrowed her forehead, giving her head a little shake in an effort to dislodge serious doubts that her family could handle a decision with the gravity of a well-chosen seat. So much could go wrong, conversationally, in the first year without their fearless leader, who ran things from the head of the table.

Though there were certain to be less disagreements without their brothers, the sisters knew how to get each other going as well. The last thing they needed was a fight. Julie had no desire to sit at the head of the table, however. If no one was in charge, they'd have to govern themselves.

"You're right, darlin," she answered in gratitude, conceding the battle to her higher self. Thank goodness for Drake yet again asking the necessary questions to help get her there.

The forks shone perfectly next to the second set of her mother's china, the good set with cherry blossoms and the wavy gold rim.

***

After Mom's passing over the hot days of the summer, Julie's own willingness to move into her childhood home surprised her. If she thought about it on her bad days, the rearranging of the pieces from this dollhouse to that felt like replacing one character with another: Mom doll, buried in the dirt. Julie doll, in Mom's kitchen.

On her good days, and to anyone on the outside, it just made sense. A big, well-appointed and cared-for house. Someone should take it over, lest this resource, this family fort, be squandered. During an era Julie considered The Big Decision Era, after Mom got sick but was living her days in a care facility, many conversations orbited the topic.

When it had been three months since they buried Mom and none of Julie's five siblings nor any of their children seemed to be seriously considering it, she woke in the dark hours of the morning from a dream about filling out endless forms, signing her name at the bottom of a stack of papers that grew bigger and wider with each page flipped. The stack would never end, and her dream hands could no longer grip the pen. She woke up in fits.

After that she lay in bed, bleary and bored, thinking of all the other changes occurring in their emptier nest, her remote work with the state, Drake's work slowing down with the college, and asked, why shouldn't it be them?

When she finally shared her mind with Drake, it wasn't hard to convince him. He had never been tied to one place in the way that her family was. He loved the idea of becoming part of the history of the town the Andre family helped build. The mere yards to walk to the general store for groceries, pour over coffees, freshly baked bread, and vegetables with dirt still on them. All of it supporting the sweet young family that bought the store from the last of the Andres to own it.

Sure they weren't the same type of small-town as Jewel's parents, but they could live their days here. They could easily travel if they got stir crazy. Their kids were used to visiting here anyway.

So they bought it. The six siblings finished cleaning it out, divvying up the stuff that wasn't staying. Julie and Drake moved their things from their Dubuque house. Drake showed up one night with the deed to their cemetery plots, and he began to think about a proposal to purchase the former school from the town to make a history museum. The thought carried him through the duller moments in meetings and yard work, and he made sure his daily walk took him past the property, right before he sat down at the old farmers' coffee table at the general store, armed with questions about land, families, weather patterns, and how things went around here.

***

Julie reveled in the golden aromas of the cold season: a distant fire blowing across the rolling farm valleys, roast duck skin, the crisp crust of a hot pie, a blanket fresh from the dryer.

Focusing on such dichotomies made the long months of Iowa winter easier. They were just getting started with the long nights of winter. She thought of field mice with their large stores. While they would feast tonight, she must reserve some of this celebratory spirit for later days, when everyone's moods seemed to be as distant as the faraway sun.

Julie thought holiday dinner should be a resting place, not a perilous adventure. Trusted sauces, textures, and seasonings provide the expectant comfort and tradition of the family meal. Though occasionally someone would try to spice things up, the prevailing school of thought was to focus on doing the old standbys and doing them well. Still to come with their guests were a host of delegated 9x12 cornflake covered horizons: green bean and button mushroom, cheese and potato, perfectly al dente elbow macaroni with cheese, corn, some kind of creamed soup.

She put a table out for desserts, a canvas for forthcoming configurations of fats, grains, and sugars. Snowy haystacks made from the branch-like strands of crispy La Choy with jeweled cranberry gems tucked in deep, the very picture of a winter wonderland. Numerous takes on the idea of the perfect winter cookie: iced sugar, double chocolate with candy cane sprinkles, a spiced and nutty double batch cut from a log, and two competing gingerbreads. Pillows of puddings and puddles of port.

Julie decided to get just a bit blurry on wine and the cyclical hope of holidays before guests arrived. She set her glass down and took in her work from earlier that morning: the silver sat gleaming and ready on the kitchen counter. In an hour it would be filled with the steaming recipes gathered from both sides of the family and from pages ripped from the glossy canon of the modern saints of secular holiday hosting: Martha, Ina, and Deb Perelman. For now, the shiny cavalry stood proud, dormant warriors with memory in their armor of past battles, differences in perspective and territory spurred by bottles and the loving, serious ferocity of family, softened by the treaty of laughter. Her eyes glistened with memory and Montepulciano.

She brushed the crumbs from her denim apron and heard the doorbell ring. Grabbing her goblet and topping it off, she opened the door to the darkening day. Two figures dashed through the freshly fallen snow to light the last candle.

Drake came up behind her with their coats and his eyes smiled wide as they looked up the street. The luminaries started at their driveway and continued all the way up the hill toward the store. Each lit paper sack invited them to walk toward the next one and eventually led all the way to the fully lighted intersection of Beaufort.

"Did you see who did this? Who lit the candles? I swear I saw you guys run to your car to stash the evidence," Julie smiled at Otto and her sister's partner who had each other in a headlock. As she made her way toward the four-way, she was joined by her slowly arriving family.

June, in an oversized wool jacket with big anchor buttons and an upturned collar, swiped her sister's glass and took a big mouthful. "Happy Solstice, Jul!" Deannie came up from behind and finished off the last swig. Her kids and their cousins were arm in arm, the little ones playing in the accumulating snow.

"Julie, who did you pay to bring this back?" Deannie probed. "Or maybe it was you all along."

Julie laughed and shook her head as she pulled her puffer over her apron, narrowing her eyes against the snow falling against the setting sun. She lowered her laugh as she approached and nudged Drake in his ribs, "Honey, was it you?" His lit-wick eyes told her that it wasn't, taking in the astonishment of it all for the first time.

Other people were starting to gather outside. Julie waved at neighbors, some she used to know and some she hadn't met, new commuting residents that had bought the affordable homes of the outgoing generation of this dying town. Most were dressed in festive garb, few with outerwear as stylish as her sisters. Someone across the way was striking up a song. The dark church looked slightly less foreboding surrounded by light, held by luminaries, though the candles led to the dark, locked door.

What was next for this sacristy and sanctuary, abandoned by the diocese but still containing the ghosts of their ancestors? What could be housed there? What brings people back, and what makes people stay. A collective magic-making. But who makes the magic?

The cobblestones that joined the cornerstones of commerce and community still lived under the practical pavement. When traffic going *through* instead of *to* Beaufort increased, they had to cover the old road with smooth asphalt. For years, people had been genuflecting at the four-way stop instead of in the pews of Holy Trinity. The candled way was proof that the spirit could still be found in their little town, even if it needed to be reshaped, renamed, or reimagined into something they would all show up for.

***

About the Author

Katrina Sogaard Anderson was raised in an Iowa small town and lives in one again. After earning an English Education degree from The University of Iowa, she taught high school in the West Town neighborhood of Chicago. She spends her present days as co-owner and operator of Mount Vernon's Little Scratch Coffee Roasters, living in her adopted hometown with her husband, their two sons, and dog Rosy.

9
WHITE ELEPHANTS
By Anne Houghton

"I still miss Grampy at Christmas. Even after all these years."

The elder lady bent her white head over the kitchen table, where she wrapped a small item in red and green paper. "We all do, Haley. You do understand that he wouldn't want us to wring our hands and be maudlin over it."

"I know. But you know we'll all remember it. What's in that one, Gran?"

Her grandmother, Carol, smiled. "Grampy's usual."

Haley, now a graduate student at the state university, grinned. "One left glove."

"That's it. Some traditions continue." The old lady held up the small package. It was wrapped so beautifully it might have been an expensive piece of jewelry, not a white elephant token.

The family holiday traditions had long included a white elephant gift exchange. Gag gifts had been their grandfather's specialty but there had been ordinary gifts too, so long as they could be found for under five dollars, which was a challenge in itself. Homemade gifts were encouraged.

A frenzied series of high-pitched barks sounded from the living room. "That'll be your folks," Gran said. She went to check on the turkey, as she knew the first thing out of her son's mouth would be a question about how long till dinner.

Haley opened the side door and stepped out to help carry in side dishes and plastic shopping bags full of wrapped gifts. She followed her dad into the house just as he asked, "What's the ETA on the turkey, Mom?"

"We're aiming for two o'clock."

"There will be plenty of food for snacking beforehand, so you won't starve, John," added his wife as she followed him through the kitchen. "Carol, the green bean casserole is ready to go in the oven. Where do you want it till then?"

"In the basement fridge, thanks, Maggie. Haley, you can put those presents under the tree."

Amid the bustle of setting out presents, the ancient dog Bubu sounded the alarm again, waddling over to the door. Minutes later a gust of cold air announced the arrival of Carol's daughter Sarah, her husband Mike, their married daughter, Laura, and her husband complete with fussy baby and sleepy toddler.

"Three hours in the car and my legs are stiff as boards," complained Mike, hobbling into the kitchen. He set down some bags on the already crowded kitchen table. "Who's peeling potatoes?"

"Don't look at me," grinned Sarah. "I'm holding Babybob." She had the baby in her arms and a diaper bag slung over her shoulder, walking right through the kitchen without stopping, leaving a heavy odor in her wake.

Babybob's parents did not mind that their ten-month-old had been temporarily stolen by his doting grandmother, especially with a dirty diaper. Laura handed their sleepy three-year-old off to her husband. "Gran, can we put Hazel down in your room? Then she can find us when she wakes up."

"That's fine. Leave the door open a crack so she can hear us when she wakes up." Carol led Laura and her husband, Andy, to the downstairs bedroom. This was Carol's room now after her children insisted she move there from the upstairs master bedroom.

Carol set pillows around the sleeping little girl, and Bubu's barking alarm could be heard yet again. The young parents tensed, watching their child stir. Carol covered her with a light blanket.

"Andrew, there's a little fan in the closet there," Carol said in a low voice. "Let's set it on the floor and hope the white noise helps her nap a little longer."

They turned on the fan and Hazel settled. "Thanks, Gran, she's been too wound-up to sleep. We'll give her an hour or so."

Carol followed Laura and Andy out of her room. The last of her grandchildren had arrived. Lucas and partner Melanie and their eighteen-month-old Ava up from Des Moines; they'd picked up Gabby in Ames. And Ben, who had travelled the farthest, from Chicago.

The kitchen had become the focus of activity. Carol's children and grandchildren were all talking over each other, hugging, bumping elbows, rubbing shoulders, and tripping over each other's feet. Bubu added to the chaos as he threaded his way among the many shifting feet, seeking handouts and sniffing the floor for crumbs.

Carol sat down in the dining room, watching her descendants all packed together in the kitchen. How had she gotten so old? She was a great-grandmother now; her children were grandparents; her grandchildren were mostly done with their schooling and were building their adult lives.

Yet they were still extremely noisy. Her grandchildren, the five cousins, all within four years of age, had had great fun together as children: shrieking and jumping over the lawn sprinkler in their swimsuits, bits of grass clinging to their bare feet; running in the dark, arms outspread with sparklers in each hand; creating imaginary worlds together, dressing in makeshift costumes; making long slow arcs in the tire swing that had hung from the big red oak, now long gone.

They had made a newspaper that had been one of the funniest things Carol had ever read. They had bickered and quarreled and tattled on each other as well. Five strong personalities sometimes in harmony, sometimes not. *O'er the fields we go, squabbling all the way.*

Her daughter Sarah reappeared, carrying now sweet-scented Baby-bob. The newest great-grandchild was named for the great-grandfather he would never meet. At first his parents were determined not to use nicknames. Only the name Robert was acceptable. But as often happens, good intentions had little to do with reality. The happy, drooling little boy had devolved from Robert, to Rob, then to Bob, finally deteriorating further into Babybob.

The old buffet was rapidly filling up with pre-meal snacks. Carol's granddaughter Gabby, an avid foodie, proudly carried in a large charcu-terie board and placed it front and center. Au courant goat cheese dip and handcrafted tortilla chips, avocado hummus, and caprese skewers jostled for space with less trendy fare: gingerbread, Christmas cookies and bars, homemade candy, and bags of chips.

"Unless you are actively helping to get this meal on the table, get out of this kitchen!" Maggie yelled, flapping her arms in a shooing motion. Everyone except Carol, Maggie, and Sarah evacuated.

"White elephant time," declared Haley. "Who's playing?"

After a few grumbles (*aren't there any games on?*), the younger generation settled in, along with their uncles. They balanced their plates laden with snacks on their knees or set them on the floor. Melanie sat down with Ava on her lap. John brought in a box and set it on the floor next to her.

"Oh, Gran brought down some toys!" said Lucas, pulling a ninja turtle out of the box. Melanie leaned in and picked up a dachshund beanie baby and a handful of Duplos, setting her daughter at her feet to play.

"Were there any Polly Pockets?" Laura wanted to know, always alert to any potential child hazards. "Oh, here's my Barbie." She stroked the doll's tangled hair and set it down by her plate. "Hazel will want to play with it."

"Yeah, but I took out everything with little pieces," Haley assured her, as she set the white elephant gifts on the coffee table.

The assembled players drew their numbers and the swap began. Groans and cheers accompanied the opening of gifts: a hula skirt, a VHS tape of *Surf Ninjas*, a jar of Aunt Maggie's homemade salsa, a stunningly wrapped Christmas cookie with a bite out of it. John held up a narrow strip of lumpy purple crochet. "What is this?"

"It's a thong!" Mike hooted.

"No, it's not, it's a steering wheel cover!" cried Gabby indignantly. Her cousins roared.

Once everyone had a gift, the swaps could commence, though other new gifts were chosen. The salsa was swapped again and again.

"Seriously, we need to change up this game," complained Ben, his blue cardigan adorned with gaudy holly leaves. "We've been doing this the same way forever."

"Why, what's wrong with it?" Lucas asked.

"Nothing. It's just time for us to try something else," said Ben, waving a hand toward the diminishing pile of gifts. "Aunt Maggie makes tons of salsa every year and she gives us jars anyway. Why is everyone trying to get this jar if she'll give us one anytime?"

He held up the gift on his lap, an Elvis calendar from 1986.

"Yes, it's funny, but I'm just going to throw this in the recycling. It has no value," he said. "I saw a gift swap game online that looked more interesting. You set a limit of twenty-five dollars or so and buy a gift that we all would actually want to own. Something decent, and they aren't wrapped so they can be displayed. We also put a few gift-wrapped bricks in a separate pile. About half of the bricks have money taped to them, like ten- or twenty-dollar bills or more. Players can choose a gift, and then once everyone has a gift, the swapping starts and the bricks are in play. If you pick a brick, then you're done with the game whether it has any money or not."

There was silence for a moment.

"That's basically a game show," Melanie declared.

"And it's mercenary!" Haley, who loved traditions the most, exclaimed. "The white elephant swap is supposed to be the opposite of that!"

"You have to admit that it's fun and we laugh a lot, Ben," Lucas, ever the peacemaker, said carefully. "If you really are bored, maybe we could add a smaller change to the rules like having everyone pass their gift to the left."

"Or if you have your gift taken three times, no one can steal from you anymore," offered his uncle John.

Ben, who had the shortest fuse, was sullen. "It was just a suggestion," he muttered. "I mean why do we do this anyway? Why do we still have a gift-wrapped left glove every year?"

"It's fun and it reminds me of Grampy!" wailed Gabby. "I look forward to this!"

Mike and John exchanged a glance. "I think it's my turn to peel potatoes." "I'll help." Both of the older men rose and left their children for the safety of the kitchen.

"No one *has* to join the white elephant swap, Ben. If you don't enjoy it you don't have to do it," Lucas pointed out.

"Oh, so you're kicking me out?" Ben's voice rose.

"It's the MBA," sniffed Haley. "Business school makes people avaricious."

"Oh really? What's your airy-fairy literature degree good for?" Ben yelled.

"Mommy!" A child's scream came from the bedroom. Hazel was awake. "I'll get her," Andy said quickly and escaped the game.

Eyeing the cousins, Melanie scooped up Ava and a few toys and followed Andy.

The five cousins didn't even notice. Now they were all standing, talking over each other. At their feet, Bubu was browsing unnoticed from plate to forgotten plate, gulping down any food he could find. Their parents stared at them from the dining room. "This is as bad as they were at Cousin Dan's wedding," Sarah said, shaking her head.

"Why, what did they do?" Melanie asked her, joining them. John rolled his eyes. "There was an open bar. By the end of the party, Gabby, Ben, and Laura almost came to blows over what is the proper technique for fighting with lightsabers."

"Lightsabers," Melanie repeated, staring at Uncle John. He nodded. "No more open bars for this crowd."

Finally, one of the cousins was driven to violence. "Ow!" yelled Ben, clutching his forehead.

There was complete, shocked silence. Andy gasped. "Laura, did you just hit Ben with a *Barbie*?"

Carol walked out of the kitchen and took in the scene. She looked at her children and then at her grandchildren. She walked to the living room and spoke quietly but with authority.

"If you are going to behave like children you will be treated like children."

***

The dining table was beautifully set. Carol had brought out her best china and silver. Crystal glasses and goblets caught the light. Tall candles in pewter candlesticks glowed. An array of delicious dishes was arranged down the middle of the table. She presided from one end of the long table, Babybob had the honor of occupying the other end.

His highchair stood on a bed sheet spread out on the floor, where Bubu sat hopefully. Babybob babbled with delight as he squeezed mashed potatoes between his fingers. Ava, seated on a booster seat next to Melanie, munched on crackers and sliced bananas. Hazel, also on a booster, sat next to Andy, taking an active part of the dinner conversation and nibbling on a wadded-up jelly sandwich.

Though there was indeed room for the five cousins, they were not invited to join the company in the dining room. Instead, they jostled for space around a card table in the living room, eating from plastic plates and drinking from plastic Tupperware cups in silence.

"So, are you and Andy going skiing this winter?" Lucas asked, breaking the ice.

"We're going to Steamboat in February," Laura said quietly, grimly sawing away at her turkey with a plastic knife.

"Are you staying at a hotel or renting a condo?" Ben asked, tentatively joining the conversation.

"Renting a condo. It's a pretty big one actually. It sleeps eight," Laura said. "Andy's cousins were going to meet us there but now they can't go. We're stuck with it. The smaller rentals were all taken."

"I love Steamboat," sighed Gabby. "Me too," said Haley. "I haven't been there since high school."

***

John brought another bottle of wine from the kitchen. He leaned over the dining room table and spoke quietly. "Now they're all planning a trip to Steamboat together."

"Are you serious?" asked Sarah. Their spouses shook their heads in disbelief.

"That's fine. They can vacation together, and quarrel all they want," Carol said. "Just not here."

She lifted her glass to the others at the table. "Merry Christmas."

***

About the Author

Anne Houghton is a retired librarian. She spends her time volunteering, traveling, and hiking. And reading; she has joined way too many book clubs.

10

ANYWHERE BUT IOWA

By Marc Dickinson

O n the eve before Christmas Eve, I finally decided to sell my gun, handing it over to a pawnshop like second-rate scrap metal. With the charges pending and the holiday on the way, it seemed like the only thing to do, so when I walked into Dexton Gun & Pawn on my lunch break, I figured I'd get a wad of cash. Instead, the broker stared at the firearm like nothing special.

A thick pane of scratched plastic stood between us. His face was slick with grease and the place smelled like dirty laundry. He didn't even bother to look up when he said, "Five hundred."

I told him it was easily worth double. Some people would probably pay even more.

"Uh-huh." He took off his fat, black glasses. "Five hundred."

Broken appliances filled the shelves. Metal bars barricaded the windows like a jail cell. In other words, the store was a real heap where you'd be lucky if a customer had a mouthful of teeth, much less a dollar to spend. Dexton used to be a nice town, until the factory closed, so now the only things left were a fully stocked pawnshop and a bail bondsman who kept plenty busy. Even today, on the way to work, I saw a boarded-up building with *No Copper* painted across the door. Lately, it all felt like a different country, something third-world—anywhere but Iowa.

"I'm coming back for this," I told the clerk, working his crossword. "Count on it."

He shrugged and reached for the register. "And it'll be right here, waiting for you."

***

Back at the garage, we were being attacked by scrooges. You know the type: tight-fisted folks with doubt in their eyes. My boss hung the sign out front—oil change and a 21-point inspection for $19.99. We all knew what these days would bring. Tons of tickets with no real money in it. Dale, the owner, would get people with a cheap bargain, then we'd try to find something else wrong. And it worked. Most pulled up with rusted-out exhaust pipes or engines knocking away like busted clocks. But the people we drew with these deals could barely afford five quarts of 5W-30. So, they'd simply tell us to *pull her around*, and we'd be stuck with a worthless estimate and a waste of time lube job.

Scrooges. They were all over the place today.

Bill was lifting up a giant F-150 that looked about two miles away from the landfill. After catching sight of me, he raised a hand and asked, "How'd it go, Carl?"

But I ignored him. Even if Bill was a nice guy, he was a bad mechanic, always flirting with the service writer—the one female at the shop—in order to get better tickets: lightweight brake work that paid two hours for one of actual labor. Plus, all his jobs returned a week later, usually on his day off, so I was the one facing angry folks wanting a free fix. Can't blame him though. To make money in this job you had to learn shortcuts—no wonder nobody trusted us.

Of course, today all I had was a list of oil changes, work we usually left to part-timers. There was nothing big to get my hands into, which was probably good since the thought of my gun under glass, waiting to be sold, was enough to send me into stupid mistakes under the hood. But I couldn't even lift a single car before the boss was already over my shoulder.

"You're late again, Carl. Now we're really backed up."

The store was Dale's baby, so he came in every day to pry. Even installed cameras in the garage, saying it was for insurance purposes, but we knew he'd sit at home and watch us, just hoping to see something suspicious. Though I suppose I owed the guy. Two priors and a suspended sentence didn't say much for me. Still, a good mechanic was a good mechanic.

"Need you to come in tomorrow," he said, tapping on his clipboard. "Get caught up."

"On Christmas Eve? I still have to get gifts for the family."

"Come in or don't come in." Dale shrugged. "You know what happens if you don't."

I didn't bother arguing, but I also couldn't resist singing "*We wish you a merry Christmas*" until the hoist made enough clatter that all he could do was walk away.

***

It was freezing in the shop, every tool cold to the touch. As dark approached, the rush quietly came to an end. Bill strolled up to my bay, saying goodnight and sorry about tomorrow.

"Need anything?"

"Lawyer is coming over tonight. Talk about the case."

The word "lawyer" made Bill sheepish, so he gave me a *happy holidays* and slipped out the back. Dale was in his office, checking time sheets. Usually I'd pop in to say bye, but tonight I left without so much as a sound—though I wasn't in any rush to get home.

Sadie would have a fit about tomorrow, even if it was only a half-day. She hated my hours, my small paychecks, thought I should demand a raise that'd never come. Last night I even heard her tell Geoff that Santa sometimes can't find time for even the best-behaved boys. So last night I pulled out the gun case, figuring it was time—not only to get rid of the evidence, but to put a weapon to good use for once, even if it meant selling it cheap.

When I walked into the house, Geoff was watching TV, some show about the X Games. He was obsessed with bikes and had no idea the day after tomorrow he'd be riding one of his own: a BMX we saw at the mall. The other half of the five hundred would be Sadie's, though I wasn't sure what to get her. She'd have been happy enough with court fees paid in full, but that didn't seem to be enough this year.

"Hi, buddy. Where's Mom?"

Geoff stared at screen, watching a kid in baggy pants fly off a dirt ramp. Then he pointed to the kitchen, where I heard my wife raise her voice: "Those kids harass the whole street."

"They're only twelve."

"Twelve going on twenty-one," I said, walking into my kitchen. Sadie, still in her diner uniform, sat across the table from a middle-aged man.

The lawyer stood to shake my hand, but I didn't like his questions, so I ignored it and said, "They'd obviously been drinking."

"That's a different issue. Assault with a deadly weapon is our concern."

"It was a golf club. Nothing deadly about that."

"The report mentions a gun. Two shots fired."

"So they lied," my wife said. "Isn't that enough to get it dismissed?"

"Absolutely." The attorney stared at his paperwork. "If you can prove it."

"Isn't that *your* job?" I said, collapsing in a chair. "Plus, it's my word against theirs."

The lawyer flipped the pages of the report and said exactly what I'd been dreading. "To be honest, with your record, you'll need more than that."

Words that made each of us avoid the other's eyes, opening up a silence that said it all.

***

During dinner, Geoff told us about his last day at school. Holiday assemblies and eating sweets until his stomach hurt. He didn't even look at his chicken nuggets tonight, but I couldn't blame him. As they say, every good boy deserves a day full of fudge sometimes.

"What are you doing tomorrow?" I asked, a way of slowly getting to the point.

Geoff shrugged, my eight-year-old looking so sad I could hardly stand it. We didn't let him go out much, the neighborhood too shady for a kid to make even the smallest of snow angels. Foreclosed homes riddled our street, the dark porches lining up like a row of busted piano keys.

Vacant lots full of trash littered the block. And there were too many troublemakers for Geoff to even find a friend, which was probably why my boy was so lonely and set apart. When I was little, even if there was nothing to do, we could at least stay out past sunset. But now it was as if that world, like all childhood memories, had become a thing of the past.

I took a sip of beer and said, "Maybe Mom can keep you company."

My wife dropped her fork to the plate with a sharp crack. "And where will you be, Carl?"

"Earning overtime. You know, keeping myself out of trouble."

Geoff moved his nuggets around, considering a bite.

"Great," Sadie said. "Maybe on Christmas you can send us a card?"

Blood burned through my body, but I took a deep breath, tried to stay focused on my son.

"Tomorrow night we'll go look at the lights." It was a silly thing to say, knowing that the only lights strung up around here were at the cop shop, the one place nobody bothered them.

"Okay," Geoff mumbled, knowing the same things we did about where we lived.

"Why do you do that?" Sadie walked to the sink and ran water.

"What did I do?" I asked, though how her body shook, it was clear she was fighting tears.

I gave Geoff a shrug, tussled his hair. When he didn't look at me, I lifted his chin and gave him a wink. But all I got in return was an empty face, those big eyes blankly gazing back.

***

While Geoff watched TV, the Christmas specials coming one after an-other, I snuck up behind Sadie washing the dishes, buried my face in her hair.

"What happened at work?" she asked.

I pressed myself against her and said, "You know Dale. He has me on a short leash."

She stared down at the greasy suds. My hands wandered around her waist, figuring it was one way to end a fight. But she quickly moved away, told me to stop.

"What's your problem, Sadie?"

"That all your problems become my problems." She scrubbed at the dark stain I'd left on her dress. No matter how many times I washed them, my hands could never get fully clean. As if the oil had forever soaked into the skin, making all they touched turn black. Then she threw the dish rag at me and said, "Clean up your own mess for once. And if this goes to court...."

I wondered what she'd say would happen next: prison? divorce? bank-ruptcy?

Instead, my wife simply shook her head and whispered, "Golf clubs." Then she sighed and walked from the room, leaving me with nothing but a sink full of dirty dishes.

***

The morning was still dark when I stepped outside. Usually, Sadie would be at work by now, serving that overlap between first and third shift, while I drove Goeff to school. But today, the house was asleep, and it was snowing, so I let the truck idle a bit, trying to warm up. And though the trees on our block were already dead, bare branches clacking like bones in the wind, at this hour, with those flakes drifting down, turning everything white, the place looked almost at peace.

In the shop, it felt nice to be alone. It'd be a slow shift, nothing one man couldn't handle. Even scrooges took a day off. But as I put a car on the lift, ready to pull its transmission—a job that may actually pay since it'd take all morning just to get the thing out—the front doorbell buzzed. Its echo ricocheted through the garage, making my wrench slip. Maybe I was still shaky from last night, images of lawyers and lost little boys sitting in my mind. But it didn't help that in the front lobby stood one of the kids from the lawsuit—with a small woman at his side.

"What are you doing here?" I was in no mood for the talk that was about to happen.

The lady looked like she hadn't slept, eyes puffed out at the edges. She wore a threadbare coat. Dirty slippers covered her feet. "My son has something to say to you."

The boy appeared hungover. In fact, with the mom gripping his arm, he looked like any other teenager: sullen and shy. Nothing like the other night when I stood on my porch and told him and his friends to get off my property. In the dark all I saw were kids by my truck, holding something shiny, which, to me, was enough to protect my home by any means necessary.

"It's nothing he can't tell me in a courtroom, lady."

"We're here to say sorry." She let go of the boy and crossed her arms.

None of us moved, and I had to wonder if this was where we'd wind up someday: my son wearing sloppy shoes and saggy pajama pants; Sadie wrapped up in thin clothes and seeming so much older than herself. "I don't hear an apology."

She gave him a nudge, and the boy mumbled a quick sorry.

"My son doesn't need any more strikes against him," she said, pulling the kid back. "And I figure you need a someone to forget what they saw. Or heard. So maybe we can make a deal."

I knew my fair share about being in trouble, but it felt unfair how some folks never had to pay the price, always looking to cut some deal to worm their way out of it.

"Maybe some kids need to learn a lesson about third strikes—and where it can land you."

I tapped a wrench into my open palm and glanced at the clock. I still had to go to the mall for the bike. Plus, now, maybe swing by the pawnshop, see if it had a set of golf clubs for sale.

"That's how you want it?" She yanked her son to the door. "You're right about this guy."

"What kind of parent are *you*?" I asked. "Letting a kid hang out with a bunch of thugs?"

"You want a fight?" she said, wearing a look only a mother could give. "You got one."

Once they left, I thought about tomorrow. How, despite the presents I planned to put under the tree, with just a word of apology I could've given my wife the one thing she wanted. But now all I had in store for her was another battle, one more war she didn't want to wage.

***

After they left, my hands couldn't stop shaking, so the thought of pulling a transmission felt almost risky, a liability that led to no other choice but to lock up shop.

At the mall, giant piles of dirty snow had been bulldozed to the edge of the parking lot, which was now packed with cars: more folks making a last-ditch effort before the holiday.

Inside, people ran around wearing ties and dresses, making me feel exposed in a grimy shirt—my name embroidered on the front for all to see. The toy store was wall-to-wall moms and dads, shoving money this way and that, trying to get whatever their kids' lists wished for. It was crazy how hard we all tried to make life special, if only for one morning. A brief moment when grown-ups could maybe feel like good parents again.

I held up the wad of cash, like some passport that'd gain me access to a little boy's bike. But when I got to the aisle, it'd been ransacked, each hook left empty.

Eventually, I flagged down a clerk and asked, "Wasn't there a BMX on sale?"

He looked at me like I spoke another language, something foreign and lost in time.

"Sir, we've been out of those for days."

"But it was here. Not long ago."

The kid removed my hand from his arm. "It's the day before Christmas."

"I know that." I gritted my teeth and held my stack of money to his face. "But maybe you have one in back. Something you've been setting aside."

The clerk smirked as if bribes were common around here, and I saw myself through his eyes: another scrooge looking for a deal. "Sir, I can put it on backorder. That's the best I can do."

Before I could say more, he was pulled away by someone else. Sweat rolled down my face, the money wet in my hands. I wandered through the store, looking for a toy any kid would want. There were all kinds of plastic creatures with missiles attached to their arms, swords jutting from fists—violent things I refused to put in the hands of my son. I didn't even know how to pronounce the names of half of these objects. So when I saw the sleds, a dozen untouched discs hanging from the wall, I grabbed two and headed for the register.

***

I wasn't sure what to get Sadie. I walked into the lingerie store, but it felt too sexy for Christmas. I browsed jewelry but, despite all the shiny stones, nothing spoke to me of my wife. She always said she didn't need that kind of stuff. Plus, if I got a diamond necklace or a fancy bracelet, the fact that she'd have one precious piece sitting there by itself in a box felt even more pathetic. Especially when I couldn't even get my own son something as simple as a bike.

The air in each store was dry, and I couldn't take the crowd anymore, but in my truck, I felt turned around, driving without direction—until finally pulling up to the pawnshop. It was locked for the holiday, so I had to cup my hands to peer into the dark window, hoping for a sign of life. It was probably a common scene, a man begging for something he'd left behind. But when a shadow started to move about inside, I knocked until the glass almost cracked. Soon enough, the broker opened the door, standing behind his metal bars.

"I want my gun back." I held out the same roll of bills he'd given me the day before.

The guy nearly grinned when he said, "I already called the cops."

Then, when he pulled the bolt with a soft click, I knew everything was out of my hands for good. And though I felt hollowed out, staring at that locked door like a kid kicked out of class, there was also an ease about the emptiness. Some strange sigh of relief that couldn't be completely denied as I walked away—trying my hardest to not look back.

***

As I entered the house, Sadie was in the kitchen trying to settle someone down. I only caught a trace of the phone call, but it was clear who was on the other end. Eventually, Dale would forgive me for bailing on work, while Sadie, on the other hand, was probably thinking the worst.

So when I saw Geoff on the floor, watching his X Games, I snuck up and whispered, "Want an early present?"

The boy's eyes perked up as he bounded from the floor into my arms. I led him to my truck and unveiled the sleds. He stared at the plastic as if it was about to bite. And there was no denying the disappointment in his voice when he said, "I like them."

"Should we try them out?"

When he nodded, I put him in the cab and swung out of the driveway. But we'd barely left our street when Geoff asked, "Isn't Mom coming?"

"Not today. It's just you and me now. Right?"

"I guess," he said, smiling. But it was easy to hear the tremble behind the words.

"What? Don't you want some guy time with Dad?"

Geoff shrugged. "It just feels like this is something a family should do."

"You've been watching too much TV."

Instead of a laugh, he scooted away to stare out the window. And though I didn't want to look, it was impossible not to see his reflection in the glass, those empty eyes slowly filling up.

By now, Sadie was probably in a panic. I imagined her calling the cops, leading to a final strike that'd take me where I'd been headed all along—for a long stretch of my own making.

So, today, when I saw the one slope that passed for a hill on our block, it felt like a last chance to give my boy a parting gift as I hit the brake and said, "This looks like the spot."

It was just vacant lot, so often choked with trash you couldn't even see the drop. But today, snow covered the garbage, revealing a small decline, pretty as a painting.

Snow was about to fall again, and the dark was coming on fast, so I tucked the sleds under my arm and led Geoff to the edge. My son surveyed the scene, as if plotting out the course, until he looked up to me as if asking for a bit of advice, something to get him through this new terrain.

"I want you to remember this day. Will you do that for me?" But before he could say yes or no, I pushed a disc into his hands. It looked huge next to his small body. We dropped the sleds side-by-side. Then I picked up my boy and plopped him onto the plastic, saying, "Hold on tight."

"Are you sure this is okay?" he said with a thread of worry. The kid knew as well as anyone that this wasn't any kind of place to fool around. I mean, who knew what kind of sharp-edged objects lay beneath all that white stuff.

"Who's going to stop us?" I said, crouching down behind him. "Ready to launch?"

"Wait. Aren't you coming too?"

I put my palms against his back, ready to shove my son down into that hole, but not before giving a promise that I'd be right there to catch him when he hit bottom.

A version of this story originally appeared in Replacement Parts (Atmosphere Press, 2024) and North American Review (296.4 Fall Issue 2011)

***

About the Author

Marc Dickinson is the author of the short story collection, *Replacement Parts* (Atmosphere Press, 2024). His stories have appeared in *Shenandoah, Indiana Review, Cream City Review, North American Review, Greensboro Review, Chattahoochee Review, Beloit Fiction Journal, South Dakota Review, American Literary Review* (as winner of the *ALR* Fiction Prize), as well as other journals. He received an MFA from Colorado State University and now lives in Iowa with his wife and two children, where he teaches creative writing at Des Moines Area Community College and coordinates the long-running reading series, *Celebration of the Literary Arts.*

11

THE 2035 CHRISTMAS PIE CONTEST

By Nick Narigon

"**A** pie contest," spluttered Bryson, flecks of spittle gleeking through his braces. "That's the stupidest thing I ever heard."

It was a cold December afternoon at East Miller Middle School. We were excited because there was only a week left before Christmas break, and it was Thursday—half-day. The superintendent recalibrated the AI K-Bot intraverse every Thursday, which meant our K-Bot teachers were dormant for the afternoon. We wore our mittens and mufflers inside school because the recalibration caused the heat pumps to also take a break.

This meant it was movie time, and we were on our way to huddle together inside the school auditorium to watch the latest K-Nova Studios flick, *Max Sinclair and The Last Algorithm*. On our way to the auditorium my friends Bryson and Spaz had been arguing about the movie. Spaz complained that *The Last Algorithm* was a clone of *Return of the Algorithm*, which we watched last week.

"What ya gotta watch is Ninja Turtles," blurted out Spaz through her red- and purple-striped scarf, her black curls springing as her head nodded excitedly. "My grampa's got this thing called a DVD player and when you push the button this metal disc goes all zoom, zoom, zoom, an' then this movie shows and it's a frickin' turtle, four turtles I mean, that do all these hyah, hyah, hyah, moves an' totally kick weasels."

"I think my dad has some Ninja Turtles comics at my gramma's house," I interjected.

"What?! No chop!" shouted Spaz in near hyperelliptic shock. "Oh… I need to see those. I love the shiny classic comics you can open 'an all and make the pages go all flip, flip, flip…."

It usually takes Spaz a minute or two to realize nobody's listening to her because by this time Bryson and I were looking at the new poster hanging outside the tech lab announcing the school's Christmas program—including the aforementioned Christmas pie contest.

Before I get too far ahead of myself, or behind myself, let me explain who I am. I'm Ozzy and I'm 13. I'm in the eighth grade, and I live in East Miller, Iowa. There is no West Miller or North Miller or even just Miller. I think there was some guy named Miller, and they built a town east of his place or something.

East Miller was a small farm town until a few years ago when K-Nova built a new data processing plant on top of the old cornfields and now we're a city with a shiny new fire station, and a swimming pool, and separate elementary, middle, and high schools. The year I started middle school, in 2033 I guess, they replaced all the teachers with the K-Nova AI Learning Facilitation Bots—or K-Bots for short.

It was kinda fun at first. They put these robots in people clothes at the front of the classroom to seem like real teachers, but all we do is look at our K-Tablets. Each lesson on the K-Tablet is customized for every kid depending on their skill level and interests.

I'm supposed to be doing algebra, but the algorithm got all out of whack and the K-Tablet spews out these advanced theorems and proofs like the Pygmy-tha-moron Theorem or something and I get so confused I can't tell if smoke is coming out of the tablet or my ears.

That's when I put the K-Tablet down and play card games with Bryson and Spaz. The intraverse's supposed to keep us from playing games or watching clicks on the K-Trax video app, but Spaz figured out a little trick. All she does is ask the K-Bot teacher some offbeat philosophical question, like, "If Shakespeare said, 'To be or not to be is the question,' then what 'bout my goldfish Andy? My sister fed him pop rocks, and the poor guy nearly exploded. Is my goldfish Andy not being now? Or is he to be?"

While the K-Bot lectured for two hours on the state of being of Andy the goldfish, Bryson, Spaz, and I played gin rummy with this faded and bent-up deck of cards Spaz found at her grandpa's house.

The only adult left in school was Superintendent Anderson, and he was too busy recalibrating the intraverse system or reattaching the fingers of K-Bots after they've been pulled off by sniggering seventh graders to do much discipline.

I guess you could say school was alright. We could have done most of our work at home, but they thought it was good for us to interact with other kids on a daily basis. I didn't think I needed to interact with Bryson every day.

The school did continue some of the old traditions like the Christmas program. They put up a tree every year. A real one. Santa came and passed out digital K-Nova stamps. The choir kids sang hyperpop Christmas carols with the DJ club.

Then there was the pie contest. There was nothing special to it. You baked a pie and the best one won.

"Who even eats pie?" cried out Bryson, stabbing his mittened finger at the poster, his spittle warming up a cloud of steam.

"I love pie," said a voice from behind us. We turned to see who it was. Oh my God.

It was Brynna Olson. The prettiest girl in school. She was talking to us. I mean, she was talking to Bryson. Fudge pickles.

"Pie!" screeched Bryson, his fresh patch of pimples turning bright red. "You like pie?!"

"I like pie, too," I mumbled.

"You do?" said Brynna brightly, looking at me, holding her sparkly pink K-Tablet to her chest, her long hair curled up around her fuzzy blue earmuffs just so, her eyes bright sparkles of wonderful. "What's your favorite?"

"Um...?" I stammered.

My brain sputtered. It whirred like the K-Bot's voice when the intraverse stalled. Then a name of a pie came to me, and I blurted it out.

"Pecan," I said.

Pecan! my brain screamed at me. *You hate pecan pie!*

"I love pecan!" gushed Brynna, a picture of beauty incarnate. "Maybe you'll make one for me at the contest."

With that she brushed against my shoulder and sauntered off without as much as a look back.

"Bah, what does she know," grumbled Bryson. "She can't even circumnavigate the K-Nova quanto processor."

"Yeah but her Trax dances are grip. She's all like this, and that, and hah, and gah," said Spaz, contorting her body in different directions. "Brynna's gets like a gazillion reactions on her clicks."

I was no longer listening to them. All I knew was that I was going to bake a pie. A pecan pie.

And I was going to win the 2035 East Miller Middle School Christmas Pie Contest.

***

That night as usual my mom came home after supper from her job at the K-Nova data processing plant cafeteria. Thanks to her job we were able to live in the K-Nova family dormitory. Mom and Dad divorced when I was little, and I don't have any brothers or sisters, so I got my own room.

I had made a frozen pizza and left half of it for Mom. When she got home, she tossed her ketchup-stained apron in the hamper and sat down at our little dinner-table-for-two in a huff. A plastic Christmas tree with a ceramic Max Sinclair figurine perched at the top sat in the middle of the table. Mom held her forehead in her hand and nibbled at the limp end of a slice of pepperoni pizza.

"I need wine," she groaned.

"I think we're out," I replied, pouring her a glass of milk instead.

She looked at the milk with dismay and took a big gulp.

"That didn't help," she sighed.

"Mom?" I asked. "Um..."

"What?" she asked, perking up, wide-eyed. "Is it something at school? Did I miss something on the app? What do they need money for next?"

"No...," I said. "Um... well, yeah... you missed the PTA signup for the Christmas grams... but... um... do you know how to make pecan pie?"

She looked at me, strands of hair falling out of her ponytail. She took a big bite of pizza.

"Pecan pie?" she mumbled through her full mouth. "What the...?"

When Mom had the time, she was a half-decent cook. It was her job after all. My birthday was in October, and she baked me an apple pie every year. It was kind of our thing. She must have known how to make a pecan pie. How different was it from apple? A pie was a pie after all. Right?

"Yeah," I said. "A pecan pie."

"What on earth for?" asked Mom after gulping down her pizza.

"For school," I said, matter-of-factly. "For the pie contest."

"Pie contest?!"

"Christmas pie contest."

"You want to make a pecan pie for the Christmas pie contest?" Mom asked, wiping pizza sauce from her mouth. "Is this required? Does everybody have to bake a pie? This is getting more ridiculous every year. I'm gonna message your superintendent Mr. What's-his-butt right now."

Mom picked up her K-Disc which was all bedazzled and had my fourth-grade picture pasted on the back. She poked at the K-Disc as she grumbled about all the stupid apps and stupid assignments.

"No," I said. "It's not required. I just... wanna... do it."

Mom stopped swiping at her K-Disc and looked at me like the AX store clerk looks at Bryson when he asks how fast the throughput is for their parallel processing.

"You...," she said, drawing it out slowly. "You want to bake a pecan pie. Just because you wanna...."

"Yeah," I said sheepishly. I could feel my neck heating up again.

"Wait," she said, setting down her K-Disc and cocking her head to the side. "Is this for a girl?"

Now my face was beet red.

"Ummm…." I stammered. My mom's face brightened like Christmas lights.

"That's so cute!" she gushed. "Who is it?"

My feet automatically made a dash for the door, but Mom called me back.

"Wait," she said. "It's none of my business, I know. Of course I'll help you. But does it have to be pecan?"

"Umm…," I said. "Kinda."

She looked at me knowingly. Then she stood and went into our tiny kitchen and reached up and rummaged through the top shelf of the cupboard.

"Aha," she said buoyantly and took down a metal file. She opened it up on the counter and leafed through like a hundred index cards. I peeked around her elbow and saw hand-scribbled notes on each of them. Finally, she pulled one out.

"This is your Grandma Phillips' recipe," said Mom, and she held out the card to me, referring to my dad's mom. "She made the best pecan pie. She made sure we all knew."

I took the card from Mom and scanned it over. It looked as if it was covered in Egyptian hieroglyphics.

"What is this?" I asked. "I can't read it."

"Oh," said Mom. "That's cursive. They don't teach you cursive in school?"

I shook my head, and Mom took the card and flipped it back and forth perusing both sides.

"I can read some of it," she said. "But her chicken scratch is worse than a doctor's."

Mom handed the card to me and returned the metal box to the top shelf.

"Um…," I said. "Can you call Grandma and ask her to, you know, help with the recipe?"

Mom put her hands on her hips and looked at me again with her head cocked. Then she leaned in and put her hands on my shoulders. Our noses nearly touched in an elephant kiss.

"Ozzy, you know I love you," Mom said softly, her voice growing stern. "And I know you should never speak ill of family, but if there was one good thing that came out of the divorce with your father is that I never have to speak to that woman again."

She dropped her hands and brushed past me to clean the dirty dishes off the table. Her lips were pursed, and the dirty dishes kept her rapt attention, signaling that this conversation was over.

"Oh… okay," I said. "I guess I'll give Grandma a call myself then."

I went to my backpack and pulled out my K-Disc, which had a picture of Max Sinclair on the back. I swiped it open and held the K-Disc up to my face.

I had never called anyone before. I was nervous and curious at the same time.

"Grandma Phillips," I said at the disc.

I could hear ringing on the other end. Finally, Grandma answered. Her nostrils appeared on the surface of the disc. I could count her nose hairs if I tried.

"I told you scammers to stop calling!" she shrieked, and she hung up.

"Grandma Phillips," I said again, putting the metal disc closer to my mouth. The K-Disc kept ringing, and Grandma never answered.

Well… fudge pickles.

***

The next day at school I had pecan pie and Brynna on the brain.

I had never been into Brynna Olson before. She's in a totally different social circle. If our relationship was a Venn diagram her circles would intersect with the cheer squad, the student council, the track team, you name it. My Venn diagram had one circle, and it encompassed me, Spaz, and Bryson. We didn't intersect with anyone.

Even though we'd gone to school together since kindergarten, Brynna had never once spoken to me, and I never considered her as a viable romantic pursuit. Though to be honest I had never romantically pursued anyone unless you count my last real teacher Miss Templeton to whom I bequeathed an envelope stuffed with candy hearts for Valentine's Day.

I knew in my head that baking a pecan pie for Brynna wouldn't win her heart, but it would get her to notice me. To these new feelings that seemed to gush through my brains like Niagara Falls, being noticed by Brynna was enough.

The K-Bot teacher was droning on about Spaz's guinea pig Porky and whether she had the ability to think and if this would therefore make her "am."

I was staring at the playing cards in my hand wondering if the queen of spades had a more rounded nose then she would look like Brynna.

"Hey Deadwood," Spaz hissed at me, flapping her hand of gin rummy in front of her face. "You gonna discard or what? We wait any longer for ya and the choppin' K-bot's gonna solve the meaning of life... and find Bryson's missing retainer."

"It's in my locker somewhere," grumbled Bryson, loudly sucking in his saliva glaring at his hand of cards. "C'mon, Oz. Make yer play. Yer like in outer space."

"It's nothing," I said, shaking my head. "Whose turn is it?"

"Yours!" they exclaimed simultaneously.

"Oh," I said, and I reluctantly discarded the queen of clubs.

"It's Brynna, isn't it?" said Spaz with a big ol' cheeky grin that revealed the gap in her teeth.

"No," I said, reshuffling the cards in my hand as my neck heated up.

"Look at yer neck," laughed Spaz. "Ozzy's in looove with Brynna. You guys gonna have your own couples dance on Trax?"

"Stop it," I whispered loudly to Spaz trying to hush her.

"Brynna and Ozzy up in a tree, K-I-S-S-I-N-G," giggled Spaz. "You gonna bake her a pie or what? If ya wanna win the contest ya gotta turn in yer pie by Tuesday. You got a recipe or what?"

"Yeah, actually," I said in my best hushed voice, slipping my grandma's recipe card out of the back pocket of my jeans. "I got my grandma's recipe... but I can't read it."

"What do you mean you can't read it?" groused Bryson, putting down his cards to catch a glimpse of Grandma's now-folded recipe card.

"It's in cursive," I said.

"Cursive?" asked Spaz, her eyes widening in excitement as a new puzzle presented itself. "What's that?"

"Look," I said, flattening the card the best I could in the middle of my desk.

Spaz and Bryson huddled over the card inspecting it like it was a bloody glove at a crime scene.

"What's it say?" asked Bryson.

"Dunno," I said.

"Let's ask the K-Bot!" said Spaz with a bright smile.

"The K-Bot?" I asked incredulously.

"Sure, why not?" Spaz said with a shrug. "That dumb tea kettle's gotta be good for something."

Spaz swiped the recipe card from the desk and marched up to the K-Bot, who was now lecturing on what a guinea pig might think about the color of its own fur and why beige guinea pigs are the best.

"Read this," instructed Spaz, holding the recipe card out to the K-Bot. Its glass eyes twitched, and its latex head tilted as it considered the piece of paper set out before it.

"Yes," said the K-Bot in its monotone voice. "It's a pecan pie recipe."

"Print it out," instructed Spaz.

The K-Bot scanned the recipe with its eyes, and the printer in the corner of the room started spooling out paper. Paper that had my pecan pie recipe.

"Genius," I muttered under my breath as Spaz retrieved the printout and brought it back to us.

"Here you go," she said, plopping the printout on my desk. "One pecan pie recipe."

"You're the best," I gushed.

"And don't you ever forget it," said Spaz with a churlish grin. "You gonna get ingredients?"

"Yeah, I'll get 'em delivered," I said, slipping my K-Disc out of my backpack.

The surface of the disc shimmered in my palm. I swiped open the K-Grab app and whispered into the disc, "Deliver pecan pie ingredients."

I held up the paper printout so the K-Disc could get a thorough scan. The delivery order of ingredients appeared on the surface. But "pecans" was highlighted in red with a line stricken through it. No pecans.

Then the K-Disc spoke in a robotic voice eerily similar to the K-Bot at the front of the classroom.

"WOULD YOU LIKE APPLE INSTEAD?" the K-Disc blared.

All of the kids, whether they were doodling on their desk or gossiping in the corner, swiveled to look at me.

Fudge pickles.

"Okay, students," said the K-Bot interrupting the din. "Open the Geography app and slide to the Persian Gulf indicator."

"Oh, shoot," squeaked Spaz. "Your K-disc got ol' Tea Kettle's attention. Well, I guess we're gonna have to learn something today."

With that we each picked up our K-Tablets and set about learning about the Bay of Doha.

It might as well have been the Bay of Pigs. All I could think about was where was I going to find pecans before Tuesday?

***

"Error E-zero-nine-nine," said our coffee maker.

"What in the fff....," cursed my mother, empty coffee cup in hand, as the coffee machine blinked at her. "For peas and chicken grease what is the problem now. What is error E-zero-nine-nine?"

"Error E-zero-nine-nine," repeated the coffee maker in that robotic voice. "Lost compatibility with water supply from the K-Breeze Topline Refrigeration Unit. Please go to the settings menu inside the refrigerator launchpad administrator and drop down the tool bar to..."

"Shut up!" screamed Mom as she jabbed her finger at the off button on the coffee maker.

Mom had to work late last night since the K-Nova data center is hosting a weekend-long conference. I was asleep before she got home.

Now it was Saturday morning and I was finished with my corn flakes. Mom was just waking up and engaging in her regular screaming match with the AI coffee maker. All our kitchen appliances were connected by the intraverse. One little glitch and the entire kitchen was in nuclear meltdown mode.

"A six-digit code has been sent to the toaster oven," announced the refrigerator. "Please type in the six-digit code on the launchpad to access the coffee maker."

"I don't have a toaster oven!" screamed Mom.

I needed to ask for Mom's help finding pecans. This didn't seem like a good time, but when was it ever a good time?

"Um... Mom?" I asked, making a show of it to rinse out my cereal bowl in the sink.

"Yes... Ozzy honey," Mom said, gazing into her empty coffee cup. She was wearing a green bathrobe with reindeer on it. Her hair resembled that of the old Barbie doll in the church charity bin.

"Do you know where I can buy pecans?" I asked.

"Pecans? What on earth do... Oh, yeah," said Mom, setting down her coffee cup and folding her arms. "Pecans. Right. You can't get 'em delivered on K-Grab?"

"Nope," I said. "No pecans."

Mom tapped her fingers on the sleeves of her robe and chewed her bottom lip. There was still a smudge of lipstick from last night.

"There is someone who can help...," she said slowly, glaring at the refrigerator like it was H.A.L. refusing to open the pod bay doors.

"There is?" I said brightly. Too eager. Cool kids don't get excited about pecans.

I sauntered into the tiny living room attached to the kitchen. Aside from the projection screen on the wall the only furniture we had was a love seat and a coffee table covered in rings left from coffee cups that managed to get filled.

Mom unfolded her arms and sighed and followed me into the living room. We squeezed together on the love seat. Mom brushed aside the long brown bangs covering my eyes. She tickled the brushy hairs spurting out of my chin.

"When did my baby become a teenager?" she asked with a pout.

I could feel my neck heating up.

"If there is one thing I can do as your mother it's help you woo this mystery girl," said Mom, adding with a sigh. "Grandma Phillips has pecans at her farm in Belvedere."

"She does?" I asked, once again excited.

"She does," nodded Mom. "She gets 'em at her farmstand every year for the farmwives."

"So grip!" I exclaimed. "Can you take me?"

"Even if I wanted to I couldn't," said Mom with a frown. "I gotta work at the conference all weekend."

I sank back into the love seat, my brain scanning for anyone who could give me a ride all the way out to Belvedere. Grandma Phillips didn't farm anymore, but she still had the farmhouse and a huge garden and a Christmas tree grove.

Some of my earliest memories are going to Grandma's farm to cut down our Christmas tree. Those trips started out happy but somehow turned into a screaming match between Mom and Dad at Grandma's dinner table and ended in a silent hour-long car ride home to East Miller.

Every Christmas since Dad left, I secretly hoped we could all return to Grandma's to chop down a tree instead of putting our meager presents around the plastic Max Sinclair tree on the dinner table. It's not that Mom and I aren't happy together. It just doesn't seem like we've ever experienced the same joy we had when we built a snowman at Grandma Phillips' Christmas tree farm.

Mom's parents passed a long time ago. Dad's dad also. Mom and I were the only family we had. The rest of the year we were all we needed. Christmastime was different. Christmas was time for family. Even if all they ever did was argue.

"You can always take the K-Bike," Mom said, stroking my hair.

"I can?" I asked. "You said I couldn't ride it."

"Well...," she said. "I guess you're old enough. Besides, means I don't gotta drive you all over this choppin' town."

"Don't use that word," I mumbled.

"But you better leave soon and don't dawdle," scolded Mom, wagging her finger at me. "There's s'posed to be a snowstorm tonight. Get home by three. Not one choppin' second later."

"Okay. You got it," I said, giving Mom a mini salute. "Home by three."

I couldn't be too sour at Mom's attempt to use the teenage vernacular. I was going to finally ride my choppin' K-Bike—the best Christmas present ever.

***

"Wow! You're actually gonna ride it...," exclaimed Spaz. "That's all head toe to the let go. Like, three-sixty degrees to sunshine."

It was later that morning and Spaz and I were huddled outside Mom's garage, which was an aluminum unit outside the K-Nova dormitory lined up with all the other tenants' garages.

One of those tenants was Spaz. We've been neighbors for as long as I could remember and we've been inseparable even longer.

Mom's mini K-Volt hatchback took up the bulk of her garage. However, tucked between the K-Volt and the back wall was my K-Bike.

The K-Bike was a normal-looking motor scooter. Mine was covered in red chrome. Dad attached a basket to the back of the K-Bike. He said when I turn 16, I could use it for a job as a K-Grab delivery driver.

He said once I'm plugged into the K-Nova system then I'd be set for life. I didn't know what that meant. He wrote all this in my Christmas card last year.

The card came with the K-Bike. The K-Bike was delivered sometime last January—well after Christmas. The delivery guy just rang the bell, told Mom to sign his K-Disc, and left us the K-Bike.

Nobody in my class had a K-Bike. I was the first. The K-Bike has advanced electric powertrains and a ninth-generation dual mode DMI system. It's as quiet as a mouse. It can go 5,000 miles on a full tank. I could drive across America and back and still have enough juice to make it all the way to Sioux Falls.

Most importantly, it goes 120 miles per hour.

"Come on come on come on let's get it outta there," exclaimed Spaz, nearly jumping out of her Doc Martens.

I wheeled the K-Bike out of the garage, and we let it bask in the noon sunlight. The skies were clear and blue. No way was there gonna be a snowstorm today.

"How do you turn it on?" asked Spaz, examining the K-Bike from all angles.

"It's touchpad," I said. "Like your K-Tablet."

I tapped the square, glossy button on the small dashboard of the K-Bike, and I heard the whir of the battery. It sounded like the vent above our microwave.

"How do you drive it?" asked Spaz.

"Um...." I said.

I had come out on random days after school just to stare at the K-Bike. I watched click after click of K-Bikes on K-Trax. I never turned it on before. Mom was pretty peeved after Dad delivered the K-Bike without her permission. I was afraid to even touch it. Now the day to drive the K-Bike had arrived. Merry Christmas to me. I wheeled it out into the driveway.

"I'm coming with you. I gotta. I wanna see your dad's Ninja Turtle comics." said Spaz. "This is the best thing that ever choppin' happened to us."

"Yeah. So grip," I said, nodding firmly. "Let's do this."

I climbed onto the bike. I pulled the helmet out of the front basket and fastened it on. Spaz climbed on behind me on the banana seat and gripped my waist.

I looked at the steering column. There was the on-off button. There was a blank LED screen. There was nothing else.

"Um...," I said. Tapping at the LED screen and twisting the handlebars this way and that. "Why's it not turning on?"

"You don't know?" asked Spaz, peering around my waist to get a look at the steering column.

"Of course I know...," I said. "Just gimme a sec. It's gotta be something here."

I kept pushing at the LED screen. In every K-Trax click I watched that's all you had to do. Push the on-off button and away you went.

"Get off," scolded Spaz. "Lemme look at it."

Spaz couldn't figure out how to turn on the E-Bike either, so we called Bryson who lived in the new dormitories across the highway. He motored over on his K-Scoot.

He could have told us over the K-Disc how to turn on the K-Bike, but he wanted to see this for himself.

"Oh my oh my oh my," said Bryson in a hushed voice, examining the steering column. "I've waited for this day."

He had brought a microfiber cloth and lovingly polished the LED screen.

"You just have to hold the button for three seconds," said Bryson, finishing his inspection of the K-Bike. "You're pushing it too fast."

"Hold it for three seconds?" I asked.

"Yep," he said.

Sitting on the K-Bike, I placed my forefinger atop the touch button. I held it there and counted to three. The LED screen flipped on.

"So grip," I whispered.

The LED screen displayed the mileage and battery storage along with up and down arrows.

"Push up to go forwards, down... backwards," said Bryson. "Nothing to it."

"I know," I grunted, my ego bruised.

I tapped the green up button and the K-Bike lurched forward. I tapped the down button, and it came to an abrupt halt.

Spaz hopped on behind me.

"Let's go!" she shouted.

I nodded and pushed the green up arrow, and we left Bryson in our dust.

After a few stops and starts in town, we were able to make it to Highway 55, which is a direct line to Belvedere. Spaz and I streamed down the highway under the midday sun. The crisp air stung our cheeks, but our huge smiles cured all.

***

When we arrived at Grandma's the sky turned gray, and the white farmhouse stood out among a sea of flattened cornstalks.

On our way down the gravel drive, we passed by Grandma's farmstand. She had baskets and barrels overflowing with carrots and onion and squash and all sorts of winter produce. I scanned the baskets, but I didn't see any pecans.

I parked the K-Bike in the courtyard in front of the old barn. Spaz squealed as chickens scattered in our wake. She hopped off and gave chase after the clucking hens.

I placed my helmet in the basket and meandered over to the front porch. The front door swung open and my grandmother appeared on the porch—a whisk broom in hand.

"What in tarnation is that thing?" she hollered in her country twang. Her head was barely taller than the railing of the porch. She was wearing faded jeans and a flowered blouse just as I always remembered.

"It's me, Grandma," I hollered back. "Ozzy."

'What's that girl doin' scarin' my chickens?" Grandma scowled.

"That's just Spaz," I said, climbing the porch stairs. "She's fine."

Grandma inspected me up and down with her eyes.

"You got big," she stated curtly. "You better eat sumthin."

Grandma gave the porch a few sweeps with the broom then beckoned me to follow her inside the farmhouse. I obliged.

The inside of the farmhouse smelled just as I remembered as well. A fragrant blend of aged pine and Grandma's potpourri. The front hallway was narrow and branched off into the sitting room and the kitchen washroom before Grandma led me to the kitchen at the back. She sat me down at a plastic dining table next to a rotary phone still attached to the wall. I absent-mindedly untangled the cord.

Grandma bustled around the kitchen and set a plate of dinner rolls and a butter dish on the table.

"Eat, eat," she said. "You're too thin."

I was hungry. Spaz and I drove right through lunchtime. I devoured the plate of dinner rolls before Grandma had time to clean her bread knife.

"What in tarnation brings you all the way out here?" Grandma asked as she poured me a glass of milk.

"Well... there's this thing at school," I said before gulping down the milk.

"Sumthin so important you drove that rocket scooter all the way out here?" asked Grandma with a scowl.

"Um... I guess it's kinda silly," I mumbled. "But... um... do you have any pecans?"

Grandma and I had the same conversation that I had with Mom and my friends when the topic of pecans was broached, and I explained about the Christmas pie contest. At first Grandma was incredulous. Then she was pleasantly shocked. Then she teased me about Brynna.

"Is this girl cute?" asked Grandma. Then her faced soured. "She's not a Hofsteter, is she?"

"No Grandma, she's not... I mean... it's nothing serious...," I stammered before trailing off. "I just wanna make a pie."

"Is she at least Lutheran?"

"No Grandma she's Catholic," I said without thinking.

"Well, you can't marry a Catholic," Grandma scolded. "You'll be eatin' mackerel every Friday."

"We're not... maybe... never mind... it's stupid," I said glumly. "I don't know how to bake a choppin' pie. It's just a stupid idea."

The kitchen was silent. Grandma had a wooden spoon in her hand. When did she pick that up?

She smacked it on the table.

"Boy," she snarled. "You're going to bake a pie, and you're going to win that damn contest."

Grandma rummaged around the kitchen cupboards and pulled a plastic sack out of a motherload bundle of plastic grocery sacks. She opened the kitchen closet and revealed a cavern of dried goods. She dove deep into the closet and hoisted out a big burlap bag. With her hands cupped together she scooped out pecans into the plastic sack.

"Does your mom still make you apple pie for your birthday?" she asked as she filled the bag til it bulged.

"Yeah," I said, nodding.

"She does. That's good," responded Grandma, tying the handles of the bag. "A little too much cinnamon for my taste... but at least you kids like it."

"Yeah. Mom bakes a good pie," I said. "She said she'd help make this one."

"Good, good," said Grandma, her face slack. "She's good enough in the kitchen."

Grandma plopped the bag of pecans on the table. She held her gaze on the bag with her hands on her hips.

"I'm sorry your dad's not around," she said, her sharp gray eyes shimmering. "He wants to... you know that... just his new family... his new baby."

My stepbrother is three now. First Dad couldn't come visit because Shelly was pregnant. Then because of the baby. Then because of the terrible twos. This year he didn't bother with an excuse.

"I know," I said.

Grandma sighed and gave me a pat on the shoulder.

"Best get on," she said. "Storm's comin."

***

By the time I found Spaz taunting the sheep in the barn, snow flurries were dusting the farm's courtyard.

"But what about the Ninja Turtles?" asked Spaz, in between her loud brays at the sheep.

I told her there was no time. I placed the pecans in the basket of the K-Bike and patted them down. I waved to Grandma, who was standing on the porch. Spaz and I hopped on the K-Bike, and we sped off down the country road til we reached Highway 55.

That's when the skies dumped down upon us. The wind whipped up. The snow flurries spun around like we were driving in a washing machine.

I couldn't see the road. Headlights of a pickup truck bore down upon us through snow. I didn't know what lane it was in. I swerved the K-Bike to the right. The truck whizzed past.

Spaz and I careened forward through the snowstorm, which was growing more violent by the second.

The battery of the K-Bike started to chug. The reduction gear caught. The bike jerked before the battery started again, and we careened forward.

The LED screen on the steering column blacked out. I jabbed at it, swerving the K-Bike. Spaz clutched tighter. The LED screen flashed on. Then it blinked a few times. It went black.

We rolled to a halt. The wind howled and the snow pelted our faces. My hair and eyelashes were coated in ice.

I jabbed at the LED screen. Nothing.

"What' wrong?" hollered Spaz. I kicked down the kickstand, and we climbed off the K-Bike.

"Call Bryson!" hollered Spaz. I nodded and took the K-Disc out from my jacket's inside pocket. I huddled over it to protect it from the blizzard.

"Call Bryson!" I shouted at the disc.

The disc shimmered, and Bryson immediately answered. He looked warm and cozy in his bedroom munching on potato chips, crumbs dribbling down his chest.

"What's goin' on?" he asked.

"The K-Bike broke!" I shouted.

"It what?" he asked.

"It broke!" Spaz and I shouted together, our heads huddled close, each of us pulling our jackets tight around our necks.

"Of course it did," chuckled Bryson. "The battery froze."

"Froze?" I asked.

"Yeah," he said with his know-it-all smirk. "Everyone knows K-Bike batteries jam at five degrees Fahrenheit."

"Yeah," Spaz sneered sarcastically. "Everyone knows that."

"What can we do?" I asked.

"Get warm," said Bryson with a shrug.

"Thanks a lot," I said, dismayed.

"For nothin'," grumbled Spaz and she tapped off the K-Disc. "Get chopped," she added.

"What do we do?" I shouted.

Just then a pair of headlights emerged from the whirling snow behind us. Spaz and I watched as a beat-up, fuel-injection farm truck from the 2010s approached.

The truck slowed to a halt. The driver's window rolled down. Grandma poked her head out.

"Get in!" she shouted.

***

By the time we reached the K-Nova dormitory the snow had drifted up to the mailboxes. There was no traffic in East Miller, and Grandma easily glided us to the front stoop of the dormitory entrance. We hustled my K-Bike out of the bed of the pickup truck, through the snow, and back into the garage.

"Guess I better come in an' say hello," said Grandma, back at the dorm entrance, brushing snow off her shoulders.

Inside we stamped snow off our feet all the way down the hallway and up the elevator. Spaz said, "goodbye" when she got off at her floor and made Grandma promise for the hundredth time that she'd mail the Ninja Turtle comics.

When we arrived at our door, adorned with a plastic Christmas wreath, Grandma rang the bell before I could protest.

"I can key in the touchpad," I insisted.

"Common courtesy," grumbled Grandma, waiting patiently outside the door.

I did the same until Mom finally called on the intercom.

"Who is it?" her voice called out.

"It's Judy," groused Grandma.

There was a pause on the intercom until it clicked off. The door slowly opened and there was Mom in her crisp cafeteria uniform, ready to leave for work.

"Sorry, Judy, what a surprise" exclaimed Mom, eyes ogling my wet clothes. "I was just getting ready for work an' left my K-Disc in the other room. Is there some trouble?"

"Besides your son tryin' to steamroll his way through a blizzard on a rocket bike?" grouched Grandma. "No, nothing's wrong. Everything's peachy."

"I'm so sorry," Mom said, her face turning pale. "Please come in. Ozzy, dry off immediately and get in some warm clothes."

I took a warm shower and changed into my track sweats. When I entered the kitchen Grandma was still sitting at the table, glowering at our plastic Christmas tree over a cup of hot tea. Mom was at the front door bundled up in a thick parka.

"I'm sorry, Ozzy. I gotta go," Mom said. "I can't be late for work."

"Don't worry," I said. "I'll be fine."

Grandma got up from the table, her coat still on.

"I'll go out with ya," she said to Mom. "Gotta get back an' batten up the barn."

Grandma came over to me and held me by the shoulders, her wrinkled face beaming.

"Bake the best damn pecan pie in the world," she growled.

I nodded my head. Grandma went to meet Mom at the door.

"Ready to go?" asked Mom.

"You got plans for Christmas?" Grandma asked her.

"No," said Mom, suspiciously. "I have the day off though."

"Come out to the farm. Chop down a real tree," said Grandma. "Family should be together for Christmas."

Mom gave me a look. My face glowed.

"Yeah," Mom said to Grandma. "Let's do that."

Then she turned to me and waved goodbye.

"Love ya!" called out Mom as she left.

"Don't break too many hearts!" Grandma hollered, following Mom out the door.

I sat in the love seat and opened my K-Disc. I swiped open the K-Trax video app. For the first time I found Brynna's page. I scrolled through all the clicks of her K-pop dances. Each of the little thumbnails had thousands of reactions.

I stopped scrolling when I saw a still photo. It was a photo of Brynna at the senior home. She had on plastic gloves and a big smile. She held a spatula with a stack of pancakes dangerously hanging off the end. "Blessed to be able to give back," read the caption. The photo only had a few heart reactions from her subscribers.

I tapped the heart button and little hearts floated over her picture.

Oh, fudge pickles. I can't believe I just did that.

***

It was Monday night. Mom was home off work. It was pie time.

Mom used the frozen pie crusts I had ordered off of K-Grab to make a chicken pot pie and for the pecan pie she rolled out a crust from scratch.

"Your grandmother'd kill me if I let you use a frozen crust," insisted Mom. I believed her.

The pie filling was easy enough to make. I mixed the eggs and butter and corn syrup and brown sugar and a few extra drops of vanilla because I liked the smell.

Then I dumped in heaps of pecan. I stirred it all together. Mom watched approvingly as I filled her pie crust with the sticky sweet pecan concoction.

The oven was preheated to three hundred fifty degrees. I popped in the pie and set the timer. We have a super loud timer that can wake up the neighbors when it goes off.

I turned on the oven light and peered through the window of the oven door. Heat vapors shimmered over my neatly crimped pecan pie.

By chop I might just win this thing. I thought.

I squeezed into the love seat next to Mom. We turned on the projector and scrolled through the movie options until we found our favorite Christmas movie, *Santa Paws*.

Mom fell asleep before Santa discovered the puppy at the rescue shelter. I started watching soccer clicks on my K-Disc. I totally lost track of time until I smelled a smoky odor coming from the kitchen.

I woke up Mom.

"How long should the pie cook?" I asked as Mom wiped drool off her lip.

"What?" she asked. "What pie?"

"The pecan pie."

She shook her head and scrubbed her eyes.

"What time is it?" she drawled.

"I dunno," I said. "Like nine o'clock."

"Oh, fudge pickles!" Mom cried. She lurched out of the love seat and scrambled to the kitchen. I followed in hot pursuit.

When we got to the oven, the timer blinked at us in red letters. "Error G-nine-eight-four," it read.

"Error my foot!" shouted Mom.

"What happened?" I asked, trying to see my pie through the oven window.

"The timer's on the fritz," Mom groused as she pushed me aside. She grabbed a potholder and swung open the oven door. Steam and the smell of burnt brown sugar wafted from the oven.

I got a good look at the pie. Instead of a golden brown it was a dark brown. The edges of the crust were charred.

"What happened?" I asked again.

"This stupid AI kitchen!" bawled Mom.

She slammed her fist, covered by the potholder, into the refrigerator door.

"Is my pie okay?" I asked.

Mom pulled the potholders tighter over her hands. She lifted the pie from the oven and placed it on a cooling rack on the kitchen table.

We looked at our scorched pie.

"It's gonna have to do," said Mom glumly.

I nodded. This family had come too far to give up now.

***

It was the day of the pie contest.

I carried the pie to school in an empty K-Grab delivery box. Spaz and Bryson teased me the entire way.

"That's the worst pie I ever seen," guffawed Bryson after I opened the box for the reveal.

"Um, I'm tryin' real hard to be positive here," said Spaz, scrunching up her face. "But I think you really screwed the pooch. That pie's as dead as my goldfish Andy."

"I know," I grumbled. I still didn't know why I didn't just throw the pie in the trash and be on with my merry life.

But I was propelled forward. I was on a mission for love... or something. A mission for something new in the least. I was on a Christmas mission.

At school, the smell of the burnt pie permeated the hallways as I walked to the auditorium for the Christmas program. Kids passing by peered at my box curiously. I trudged on.

After the superintendent's speech and the lighting of the Christmas tree, the K-pop dance crew performed to J-Sauvignon's EDM version of *White Christmas*. Brynna was front and center. The auditorium went wild after they pranced off the stage.

"Okay, thank you. That was very nice," said Superintendent Anderson taking the stage. "Next, we have the... um... pie contest. Did anyone enter the pie contest this year?"

One of the K-Bots rolled out on stage and handed Mr. Anderson a slip of paper.

"Okay," he said, reading over the paper. "Will Ozzy Braxton please come to the stage."

I stood up with my pie. This was it. I felt numb as I walked to the stage. There was a long folding table set up. I placed the K-Grab box on the table. I opened it. I took out my pie. I had tried to scrape off the worst of the burnt parts, but it was still a charred, sad little pie.

I held it up for everyone to see.

"Okay," said Mr. Anderson, holding the mic, looking at my pie. "Thanks Ozzy. Anyone else?"

The auditorium was silent. The K-Bot shook its head at Mr. Anderson and said, "No."

"No?" said Mr. Anderson. "Well then. Congratulations, Ozzy. I guess you win."

That was it. I won. It might as well have been first place for being the biggest nerd in school. Mr. Anderson hung a blue ribbon with a medal around my neck. I looked at the medal. It had a picture of a pie. There were a few polite claps. Spaz hooted and hollered like the rooster in Grandma's barnyard.

"Way to go, Deadwood!" she cheered.

I smiled and my face turned scarlet. I put the pie back in the box and exited the stage.

"Okay," announced Mr. Anderson as I walked off. "Now we have the Arabic Club performing 'We Three Kings.'"

Safe in the wings of the stage I found the biggest trash bin I could and dumped in the pie.

"Congratulations," someone said. I turned to find Brynna. She smiled. She was smiling at me. Her face was coated in bronze foundation, and her eye shadow was brushed over her eyes in deep shades of purple and blue. She wore a warm-up suit over her leotard.

"Umm... sorry," I stammered. "What?"

"Congratulations," said Brynna. "That's so grip you won."

"Yeah," I said sheepishly. I wanted to dig my pie out of the trash. "So grip."

"I bake a pecan pie every year with my grandma," said Brynna. "But this year we can't. She's at the senior center. She has Alzheimer's... So, we can't..."

Brynna brushed a tear from the corner of her eye.

"I'm sorry," I said. "This was my grandma's recipe. She helped."

"That's wonderful," said Brynna, her smile radiant, her eyes glistening. "We all need grandmas... especially at Christmastime. That's like Grandma's time to shine."

"Yeah," I said with a chuckle. The lump in my throat was easing up. "I get to have Christmas with my grandma for the first time in, like, years."

"That's totally grip," said Brynna, and our eyes locked. I quickly looked away.

"Yeah," I said. "So grip."

"Well... you know... St. Pat's is having a bake sale on Christmas Eve," said Brynna. "Maybe we can make a pie together?"

Oh dear Lord, I thought.

"Yeah," I said, feeling my cheeks burn up, my lips working on their own accord. "Sure."

Brynna gave me a big smile. The glitter on her cheeks sparkled like a Christmas star.

"But..." I added. "Maybe we can make an apple pie?"

***

About the Author

Hayseed Press co-founder Nick Narigon is a graduate of the University of Iowa School of Journalism. After working as a journalist and editor in America and Japan, Nick moved to Singapore where he pursued his dream of writing a novel. He helped found Hayseed Press in 2024 to help Iowa's talented writers pursue their own dreams. Today Nick lives in New York with his wife and two sons.

12

THE FAILURE'S CHRISTMAS GIFT

By Peter Boylan

The silver-haired man stood on the top step of the Iowa Memorial Union, just inside the glass doors that look south onto Hubbard Park and watched the morning snow sift down onto the grass.

It was 37 degrees at 8:15 a.m. on the Monday after Thanksgiving break.

The maple trees along Madison Street held onto the last clumps of their red leaves, now heavy with the snow.

The students and faculty that were back for the final push of the year moved around him with the natural lethargy that follows a four-day weekend of traditional American excess.

Professor Ret Nalyob, 50, was thankful to be back in Iowa City.

A week had passed since Ret, who built a career espousing the virtues and sins of American fiction around the world, saw what had to be his final chance at creating a family collapse in spectacular fashion.

Ret was divorced, childless, and alone and slipping into the madness of middle age. The next times never happened. His friends married and had children. His younger sister gave his parents a grandchild.

Ret's maternal grandmother, steeped in the traditions of Filipino families from the old world, thought he was a failure for never creating life or keeping a wife.

She told him so on Christmas Eve, right after he got divorced.

"You have the good job. But what of your life? No wife. No children. Look at all your cousins," she gestured down the hall of her home that December night. "Families. Kids. You are a failure."

He tried to remind himself that Americans were getting married and having kids at the lowest rates in nearly a half-century. Japan had the lowest birth rate on planet Earth. His cousin's son struggled with eating crayons and was addicted to YouTube and RoBlox.

Humanity had moved on from the nuclear family as a symbol of evolutionary hope, but Ret could not re-write his genetic code nor alter his angst.

He saw solitude before death as his only future, confusing for a man born into a large family who was familiar with all kinds of love.

His accomplished friends, the ones who founded families, had kids and distributed holiday cards that portrayed stable domestic lives, warned Ret well in advance of his latest breakup.

That failure's name was Rinash, a 33-year-old model of French and Persian ancestry who whipped her way into Ret's life two years earlier as her acting career warmed up with roles tied to successful social media marketing.

Rinash was not an actress—her studio told the world—the world was living in Rinash's movie. That worldview did not turn out as Ret liked it.

He was teaching a summer course at an American school in Paris, lecturing on post-World War II American fiction's value to guide, discourage, or confound in a world increasingly devoid of American leadership.

Rinash was researching an upcoming role as a graduate student studying abroad.

Her straight brown hair tumbled below her shoulder blades, a dimpled face perched atop a frame of long, wiry muscles. She marched through the City of Light with the performative violence of a runway model.

When Ret met Rinash he had been divorced from his first and only matrimonial attempt for about five years.

He once possessed the casual stance of an athlete or seasoned performer, always quick to fit whatever frame the moment or the people in it called for.

Now he stood hunched by middle age, bowed by a midsection shaped by an affinity for alcohol and steamed rice.

His brown eyes, once sharp and tinged with grey, used to lock on whoever he engaged. The eyes were still brown and rimmed by grey, but they hid beneath bushy brows that had not been trimmed on a face that drooped around a jaw line once sharp with promise.

If anyone looked Ret in the eye these days his gaze darted downward, always away from scrutiny.

He didn't feel like very much of anything and knew people knew that.

Ret was no match for the three-time Cesar Award winner.

When they met, he was focused on finishing Hemingway's buffet, a walking tour of the American author's favorite places in Paris, as detailed in *A Moveable Feast* and other short stories just not the Ketchum, Idaho ending.

She found him on a warm summer evening sitting alone outside of Les Deux Magots, beneath the white and green trimmed awning on the Pl. Saint-Germain des Pres in the 6th arrondissement of Paris' Left Bank.

He knew she was the beautiful actress from his class.

Her agent emailed him a week before the course to let him know her attendance was purely performative and Ret need not grade whatever work she submitted. Rinash thought her attendance was work so the arrangement was easy.

She sat down at his table without an invite, navigating the late afternoon cocktail crowd with winks, and smiles, and silent "hellos" that should have terrified Ret. The conversations of the tables around them turned into soft, clinking dim.

She was wearing jeans that fit her form, sandals and a white blouse. Rinash hung her purse on the back of an empty chair and sat down across from Ret. She picked up the remnants of his martini and downed it, olives and all.

"How may I make those sad eyes smile?" she said in French, as a mother with her two children at a table nearby rolled her eyes along the Arc de Triomphe.

Ret was sitting partially slouched so that the top of his belt buckle cut into his gut while he read and drank. He didn't speak French, but it sounded pretty. And Ret was ugly and older and alone.

He woke up one day and was closer to 50 than having a family. Ret wrestled with the reality that he missed the life he always assumed he'd have. His therapist confirmed that an alarming number of men age 50 and older are tormented by the children they never had.

So strong was his immaturity and ignorance and so weak was his grip on excess that he stumbled through his 20s and 30s juggling professional successes with personal failures.

Most of that was his fault. Ret chased jobs, good times, and partners who were poor matches for him and his lifestyle that bounced between social creature and brooding recluse.

The life of a lecturer on the international university circuit was fluid and each new city, continent school, and country seemed like a path to success.

At 29 he built his base in Washington D.C. and spent five years working on Capitol Hill for members of Congress who embraced bipartisanship, before he saved enough to secure a loan for the condo on Columbia Road in the Northwest corner of D.C.'s diamond.

By the time Ret knew what success meant to him, every city seemed to get bigger and less familiar, and all he wanted was home, his home.

Ret tried to have something, but he didn't know how.

And he knew the pretty actress didn't pick his table that summer evening because of him. His thinning hair was hidden beneath a red Washington National's baseball cap, a curly W in bright white letters. He had on cargo shorts, running shoes with ankle length socks, and an Iowa T-shirt.

Rinash was beautiful and she wanted something, likely an experience that could inform her next performance. Ret, drunk with vodka and hope, ignored his instincts.

A bottle of sancerre and a dozen fresh oysters later and Ret had a remarkable connection and promises of a family-filled future.

***

"It is my hope that the children will have your eyes," she whispered to him two years later, on that horrible November day that started his sojourn back to Iowa.

Ret was dropping Rinash off at a public radio interview at an international film festival forum in Washington, D.C. in the 1100 block of Capitol Street. The segment was focused on the French cinema.

She kissed him on each cheek as she always did before leaving him, turned away from the car, and glided to the trio of double glass doors marking the entrance to the studio.

Ret recalled smiling as he pulled away from the studio and out into traffic. He remembered relaxing in a momentary mix of happiness and safety and optimism.

He hummed "La Marseillaise" as he scrolled through the FM channels for Rinash's hit.

"....and we'll be right back with the beautiful Rinash after a word from our sponsors....," boomed the host's voice, Rinash's bubbly laugh preceded a "merci" in the background.

But the corporate soundbites never played. The mics stayed hot.

"...I cannot wait to get you away from that old man to the bed where you belong...," boomed the host, Marcel, a Frenchmen so fit, well dressed, spoken and cultured that Ret always assumed he was gay.

"...*Je taime mi amor*...papa has a conference in Tokyo next week...same place as last month?" cooed Rinash.

"...the fossil does not wish you by his side?" asked the suddenly straight Frenchman. "Without you...he looks....well he sags...it is ugly, no?"

Rinash laughed, and so did Marcel.

The next sound was of a man kissing a woman and the woman liking it. The passionate noise made by lust and a life falling apart echoed through Ret's car.

Ret turned the radio off and drove home in silence. He walked out of the elevator and turned left down the hall toward his second story condo in the Adams Morgan neighborhood of Washington D.C.

Outside the intersection of 16th and Columbia Road hummed and honked with the evening rush hour.

Ret walked into his dark apartment and sat on the couch. He decided to watch TV. The news would work.

A dopamine stimulant, new data, images to fill his mind with anything but the sound of his life falling apart on an international public radio show. Ret squinted in the dark, looking for the remote control.

He found the clicker on the floor by his feet, next to an empty takeout bag from Momiji, a Japanese restaurant on H Street. He pressed the power button and let his body sink into his couch.

"Lastly tonight, heaven help the man who found out his movie star girlfriend was *Pas Bon* as they say in her country," giggled a purple gown clad anchor. "WWLD brings you this video submitted by a viewer of the moment popular literary lecturer Ret Nalyob found out the 2024 Cesar Award winner, known to her fans round the world as Rinash, was making another man's croissant rise on a radio broadcast airing live in thirty-three countries."

The image of the anchor was replaced by footage from hours earlier.

A side profile of Ret sitting in his grey, 2016 four-door Hyundai, filmed from a car that must have been to his right at the stop light.

"Yo this guy is CRUSHED," laughed a man's voice, the sound of Rinash's betrayal filling the interior of his car.

"Cuckold of the Year nomination," gasped another man's voice, choked through laughter from the same car.

The purple gown clad anchor came back on the screen.

"Sorry Ret. This is not your night baby. And for all you momma's out there raising baby boys, do not let your little men get played like this... back with weather and sports after this word from our sponsors...."

***

Professor Joel Kathy saw the memes of the news footage mocking his former student as he sat in a coffee shop overlooking the red sidewalks and the grey street in the 400 block of South Linn Street in Iowa City.

Kathy read the polished statements produced by Nalyob's dean, explaining that the popular lectures delivered by Ret were delayed as the scholar worked through personal matters.

Kathy remembered a brash, opinionated, youth who sourced his identity directly from his large Filipino-Irish family.

Kathy and his family rooted for Ret from afar, hoping each new social media post revealing a new partner would be the one that ended in a holiday card.

He knew the madness and isolation that consumed Ret in middle age.When Rinash's other man debuted on public radio he hurt for his friend and quickly paid his wife the "easiest $100" she ever made.

Professor Kathy would help Ret recover. He would bring Ret back to Iowa, where he was young man once and had hope, and maybe Ret could have that again.

Kathy took out his phone and sat in the brown rocking chair in the corner of his living room and tapped out a long message.

When he was done, he called his former student.

"Come back to Iowa and teach The Last Class," he told Ret by phone, as Ret sat in the dark in D.C. "There is still something to look forward to here. Maybe you can find it."

The Last Class was exactly that for a handful of undergraduate students. It was four credits earned through five weeks of class that ended on Christmas Eve. Only fifth year seniors were eligible.

The university asked the students to pass two exams, take weekly quizzes, and submit a final paper.

Ret told his former teacher *no, thank you*. The person he becomes when he is betrayed isn't worth anything to anyone.

One of the best parts about being divorced, childless, and alone is that Ret didn't have to ruin anyone.

Ret was best left alone to cry and drink and regret. "That could easily take me through the new year," Ret told his teacher.

In reality, the sadness was his life. The friends that once filled his nights and weekends grew up, years ago.

The dinner parties, tailgates, and live music Mondays gave way one day to soccer practices, violin recitals, and play dates between families. Ret's friends always made him feel welcome. "Uncle Ret" was invited to every toddler's birthday party. They told him how lucky he was to be unattached.

Al Pacino and Robert Deniro welcomed children as octogenarians. There is hope for you Ret, they would chant.

Having hope and having kids is much easier for the young and the academy-award-winning wealthy.

Ret thought about the professor's offer as he stood in his kitchen that night for dinner.

His refrigerator door was barely visible anyway. Blocked by the faces and vacations of his friends' families, packaged, and presented as holiday cheer.

Ret tried to focus on what mattered most to him in this, and frankly most, weekday moments.

Had he finished the shepherd's pie special from Murphy's on Sunday?

If he had, Ret remembered that it was meatloaf Monday at The Diner, a counter friendly spot a few blocks from his house on 18th Street that would serve him steamed rice that the cooks made for themselves but didn't list on the menu.

Meatloaf Monday was popular with the families in the area this time of year as parents opted for a few meals out before the crush of preparation and gathering that defined the December holidays.

Ret ate alone. Once an outgoing man happy to talk with anyone, Ret preferred silence and people watching in restaurants.

The guy eating alone at the bar has a fantastic perspective, Ret learned. I get to see everyone, and no one sees me, especially not the bar tender after his third glass of Pinot Noir.

When he was home in Hawaii, dinner was always with his parents, now in their 80s, or with his sister and her husband and daughter.

Sundays he was blessed to be with them in a backyard bounded by tropical flowers, their purple, yellow, and red hues highlighting a canopy of green trees grown by Ret's mom.

Ret thought about the parents and their kids that would walk into The Diner for meatloaf Monday.

A glass or bottle of wine often focused him away from regret and on his meatloaf and steamed rice, gravy on the rice.

Ret called Professor Kathy and said he'd be in Iowa City on Monday.

After he hung up Ret felt better knowing he would soon be alone in a place he knew that no longer knew him.

Perfect, he thought, as he reached for the black plastic box that held his leftover shepherd's pie. He took off the lid and placed it on the counter next to his microwave. He tore a square of paper towel and ran it beneath the water from his sink then draped it over the top of the container with his shepherd's pie and put it in the microwave for two minutes.

The glass plate rattled as it rotated inside the microwave and Ret thought about where he would eat in Iowa City.

***

Ret hailed from a large family, his mother a Filipino woman from a community on Oahu's west side. She made Ret with his father, an Irish guy from Chicago she met at the University of Hawaii.

His family was big and Hawaii, like Iowa, believes in family as a set of values and a way of life.

Sunday dinners, holiday parties in backyards under blue tarps with folding tables and chairs. Aunties and uncles, married for decades. Each year brought new births and the Nalyob tree branched out further.

Ret clutched the cup of coffee in his right hand, hoping the caffeine would ground the jet lag and increase his courage.

The steam fogged the wire-rimmed glasses that hung on his once angular face, now rounded by time, wine, and too many take-out meals.

He worked his neck around the stiff collar of his shirt and shifted his tall frame from left to right, moving his feet back and forth on the stairs, trying to make his shoes fit.

He forgot how cold Iowa City could be. It seeped through the wool layers and dried out your skin.

In his left hand, Ret held a dark brown leather satchel, worn at the handle and the four corners where it always rested.

In it was a syllabus, handouts, books, and other course materials he failed to review during his flights from D.C.

He raised his quad shot latte to his lips and welcomed the caffeine.

Ret walked out of the IMU, crossed the parking lot, and started down the grey concrete path past the Danforth Chapel to the English Philosophy Building.

Walking underneath the train track, Ret looked at the unlicensed artwork scrawled on the cream-colored walls of the underpass.

A brown brick, rectangular structure on West Iowa Avenue, the English Philosophy Building fronts a large parking lot behind the main library.

Professor Kathy was waiting for Ret under the brown awning in front of the double glass doors on the first floor of the EPB.

He saw Ret shuffling across the street. He appeared depressed but well-dressed.

"Professor Nalyob, a pleasure to see you again young man," boomed Kathy, who still possessed the deep baritone of a man who spent Sunday's spinning the jazz classics of Big Band era with a healthy helping of Coltrane on Iowa City's public radio station.

When he was sad, which was always, nostalgia was an elixir as helpful to Ret as alcohol.

Professor Kathy took Ret back to a time—back to the late '90s—when his writings at Iowa were lauded.

It was a course on the fiction of South Asian and Middle Eastern authors, think Jhumpa Lahiri and Edward Said taught by a Black academic disc jockey from Des Moines.

The flannel patches on Kathy's corduroy jacket reminded Ret of patterns sewn by his Filipino grandmother.

Ret walked toward Kathy on the Monday after Thanksgiving break as much more than a has been. Ret wasn't anything more than what Kathy found in that graduate class. He was just older, and fatter, and hopeless.

The professors of letters exchanged a firm handshake and a hug before Kathy walked him through the double glass doors, up the stairs to the second story, and down the hallway to his class.

Kathy talked the entire time, running through the names of the seven students enrolled in The Last Class who were trying to complete their undergraduate degrees.

Dale, from Ottumwa was a civil engineering major who realized in October that he was leaving for a design fellowship in Japan without accumulating enough credits.

Daniel transferred to Iowa from Illinois and was finishing a fifth-year double major in American Studies and History ahead of a graduate school assignment in London.

The others, three ladies and two gentlemen, had varying academic and social needs, Kathy explained, and their enrollment was motivated by unforeseen circumstances outside of their control.

Ret took that to mean they were messed up like him, and his job was to reveal one of life's coldest truths. No one cares what happened to you. What are you going to do now?

Kathy shook Ret's hand and placed his left hand on his shoulder.

"Teach them what they need and what you need in this moment," Kathy counseled before turning to leave.

Ret walked into the class, put his bag down on the grey table in front of the white board and walked over to the windows overlooking the library parking lot.

He was staring out at the black asphalt, counting the white lines that marked the stalls when the students started to arrive.

A piece of white paper with each student's name next to square boxes listed under each day of the week sat on a table by the door.

Ret asked them each to check the box next to their name under Monday. When they were done, he picked up the piece of paper and read the names out loud.

When he was done taking roll, Ret asked each student to tell him what landed them in The Last Class.

"I'm here to help you finish something really important at this moment in your life," he told his charges. "I'm here to show you that if you woke up this morning and made it here then you have a chance to be happy and successful."

Ret didn't believe a word of it. Selling hope he did not have was easy.

Dale from Ottumwa shot his right hand in the air as he bent down to the left of his desk and pulled a yellow legal pad from his bag.

With the precision Ret hoped would be applied to the construction of a bridge one day, Dale from Ottumwa walked the class through the online enrollment glitches spurred by spotty WiFi in his hometown of 25,000 people and detailed how a man more comfortable inside of an Excel spreadsheet or a Desmos application didn't read the last three pages of the registrar's manual marked mandatory in bold red letters.

Daniel from Illinois was next.

A lean young man with brown hair and black eyes, he followed his high school sweetheart to college in Illinois, a decision he ranked up there with drinking and driving.

The other six students relaxed listening to Dale and Daniel detail their plight. So did Ret.

***

Friday After Class was a tradition that defined the end of the school week for Ret when he was a young student.

The bars and restaurants in the cobblestone section of town slashed their drink and food prices by half in some spots.

One popular location featured two dozen tables covered in green upholstery lined up in three rows.

They served $5 burger baskets with fries and $5 steins holding 32 ounces of draft beer between 3 and 6 p.m. every Friday.

On the first Friday After Class since his return to Iowa City, Ret walked up Iowa Avenue, across the street and onto the sidewalk leading past the golden dome of the Old Capitol on his left.

The familiarity he sought was located on the 100 block of East Washington Street, two storefronts past a Mexican restaurant renowned for their service of burritos and quesadillas well past 2 a.m.

It was a little after 3 p.m. when Ret approached the green arched awning featuring the bar's name in white letters.

The burger baskets he came to love as a 17-year-old first year student were now $11.99 thanks to patties from Argentina. The 32-ounce draft beers were still $5.

Ret was excited for a burger basket, medium rare with Swiss, cheddar cheese, and a side of barbeque sauce.

It was dim inside, with the light coming from lamps suspended above each booth with green shades made of stained glass framed with copper wiring.

Ret climbed the four stairs in two steps and gratefully took the last seat at the left corner of the bar. A flat screen TV mounted behind the bar was mute as baseball highlights played.

Lee Jen Lan stood 5'10", her long legs disappearing into a pair of jean shorts.

A green T-shirt, with the name of the bar spelled out in white letters, was tucked into her shorts.

Her black eyes shone bright against her cream-colored face, which was tilted to the right as she considered a menu. Lee Jen's long black hair was up in a ponytail.

Ret had not seen her since the writers' conference in Shanghai, the last time they were together, about twenty years ago.

Lee Jen was an accomplished poet as an undergrauate in Hawaii who spent a summer in Iowa City as part of the programming for Iowa City's designation by the United Nations as a City of Literature.

A waitress carrying two steins of beer, one in each hand, walked up to Lee Jen and stopped to say something.

Lee Jen's face lit up with a smile, the real kind of smile, something she managed to wear often.

The smile took Ret back to the time they shared together in Honolulu. The time they fell in love.

They would find one another at after parties when Fridays turned to Saturday mornings and their friends went home. She once found him lying in the street beneath a streetlamp on the slopes of Diamond Head.

But the same skills and qualities that gave Ret a globetrotting career also made him miserable to manage on a daily basis.

The family that Ret wanted so bad required a man willing to grow roots that could only grow with compromise and care.

There is no such thing as a good man alone in a bar, he is just a man alone in a bar, Ret's grandmother's words echoed in his head.

You suck the air out of every room, Lee Jen had told him when she left the rooftop restaurant where she found him drunk and holding court near the Bund in Shanghai some two decades ago.

You live for what you want, hoping it all works out, were among the last words she said to him, the others were swear words and regrets.

Lee Jen saw him sitting at the end of the bar on East Washington Street in Iowa City and put the menu she was reading down.

She reached beneath the bar into a cooler and pulled out a chilled stein and filled it with a pilsner.

Without a word she placed it in front of Ret, stared at his shaken, shocked expression, turned, and walked away.

The waitress that made her smile a moment ago asked Lee Jen if Ret needed a menu.

He won't be honest until he's drunk, Ret heard Lee Jen say as she walked to the back of the restaurant and disappeared into the kitchen.

The waitress looked at Ret and her face shown with recognition.

"You're that guy the French actress played!" said the waitress, snapping a pic with her phone. "You are foul famous," cackled the waitress.

Ignoring her, Ret stared after Lee Jen and sat in silence.

Lee Jen was a careful, consistent person who planned her life and behaviors with precision and respect.

Ret stared at the condensation rolling off the side of his stein. He had come to Iowa City to escape five decades of disappointment.

Instead, Ret found his greatest failure, and she still hated him.

He remembered Lee Jen's easy smile shining for him long ago as they shared Korean cold noodles or scrolled through the day's sports schedules and point spreads, searching for a winner.

He lost a lot that drunk night in Shanghai.

The crowd in the restaurant had grown and the sound of students excited at the weekend's prospects drowned out the voices in Ret's head. He drained the stein and asked the bar back for another.

Daniel from Illinois walked into the restaurant and saw Ret leaning on the bar, his right hand on his stein, staring at the soundless screen playing sports highlights.

Daniel took his backpack off and sat down next to Ret.

"Thank you for taking the time to talk about my final project, I appreciate the invitation," Daniel told him.

Ret looked at his student and remembered.

He remembered Thursday's lecture about America's identity and the Constitution and Ray Kroc's capitalist vision and how he morphed that into a treatise on the virtues of the burger basket and day drinking.

No office hours this Friday, he told his students.

"If you need me, you find me at Friday After Class. More can be learned about life in a bar from its patrons than by studying the grand designs of sober men," Ret preached.

A small amount of edible cannabis played a role in Ret's remarks.

Daniel took out his laptop, and a blue spiral bound notebook and opened both on the bar in front of Ret and started talking about his final project.

"I never knew my father," Daniel started, "and his absence created a vacuum that left me questioning what I was worth to anyone."

Terrific, thought Ret, *another deadbeat who was lucky enough to create a kid that turned out good.*

It was a hard thing to see a young man, good looks, and potential buffered by youth, question himself because of some man who didn't deserve him.

Facts registered better with Ret than his students' names and according to a November 2019 report from the U.S. Census Bureau there are more than seven million men in the U.S. who fathered minor children but didn't raise them.

Daniel was one of them and as he continued his story Ret found himself sobering up.

He paused Daniel's presentation and asked a waitress to seat them in a booth to the back of the restaurant, away from the noise of the bar. Ret ordered a cup of coffee and continued to listen.

Daniel's mom worked as a waitress, bartender, barista, real-estate agent and in any job they needed her to while pursuing a master's in behavioral health.

Daniel was better off without his dad, she told him. His grandparents moved to Des Plaines, the suburb of Chicago where his mother gave birth to him.

Ret's grandparents were a daily presence in his childhood, and he understood what a gift that generational connection was.

Daniel's grandparents told him they loved him every day. His grandfather taught him to fly fish, throw a baseball, and learn how to drive.

His grandmother did the crossword from the newspaper with him and looked over his math homework. She was stern with the tough stuff but loved on Daniel more than some absentee dad ever could.

She was always at his mother's side through her daily routine of preparing meals and keeping the house in order for a schoolboy and her parents.

Daniel showed none of the signs of a young man who lacked a healthy male presence in his life. Ret envied him.

At 20, Daniel, the son of a single mother raised outside of Chicago by her and her parents was more put together and confident than Ret ever was.

As the teacher and his student that needed four more credits to move on kept talking, Lee Jen watched from the server's window in the kitchen.

She could not hear what Daniel and Ret were saying but their body language suggested a connection.

Lee Jen reached into her pocket and took out her phone. She opened the camera application and zoomed in on Ret and Daniel's table.

After taking the picture, she attached it to a text message and sent it. Moments later her pocket vibrated.

Lee Jen took her phone out and smiled at the heart emoji attached to the picture.

It's time, Professor Kathy replied.

The project is essentially a letter to my dad, Daniel concluded.

"There is a guy out there who doesn't know I exist. Maybe he will one day, maybe he won't but my life isn't defined by his loss," said Daniel.

"Did you ever ask your mom to meet him?"

"Yeah, but she never wanted to hear that," said Daniel, "She told me he was not ready for me. I asked a lot when I started playing Little League. I was the only kid on the team without a dad. My mom pitched to me in the father-son game."

Daniel finished his burger and asked Ret how he should end the project for his dad, what should he say about his life that he hadn't outlined in the pictures and the vignettes and the slideshows they had gone over that afternoon.

"You are the greatest outcome that man could ever hope for," Ret told him. "You are you because of you and your mom and your grandparents and you are incredible."

Daniel started to cry. Ret stood up and hugged him, wishing he could squeeze the uncertainty out of Daniel and replace it with the love Daniel deserved.

"Project looks good kid," said Ret.

Lee Jen watched from the kitchen as the two men shook hands and Daniel packed up his belongings and left.

When Daniel had gone, Ret motioned for the waitress and asked for his check. He leaned back in the booth and looked through the restaurant at the sliver of East Washington Street now lit up by streetlamps.

Lee Jen brought his check to the table and sat down across from him. "What are your plans for Christmas Eve?" she asked.

"I'm having dinner with the Kathys," Ret replied, staring past her out onto the street where Daniel disappeared a moment ago. "I'm going over early to help clear those maple branches that fell in their yard and help them cook."

He didn't feel up for a lecture about how bad of a man he was.

"So are we," replied Lee Jen. "My parents are driving down from Des Plaines."

Ret turned to face Lee Jen and saw the smile he thought he'd never see again.

"We can't wait for you to spend your first Christmas with your son, Daniel."

***

About the Author

Peter Boylan was born and raised in Honolulu, Hawaii but credits his career as an ink-stained wretch with five years in Iowa City, Iowa, allegedly as an undergraduate English major and one-time Daily Iowan correspondent. Boylan dedicates his days to chronicling crime in Honolulu.

13

THE CHRISTMAS QUILT

By Rachel Coltvet Kristenson

Marja crumpled to the kitchen floor, her back sliding down the cupboard doors, quietly sobbing. The *kringla* was hot out of the oven and burnt. Again. Grandma's recipe card did say in her flowery calligraphy: "Bake 5-7 minutes in 500°F. WATCH THEM."

"Who has time to watch kringla bake when there's so much more to do, *Mormor*? I wish you could be here to help me," she mumbled through her tears, calling on her mother's mother, Tavia Ellertson. It was 11:48 p.m. on December 23, 1982, and Marja Hanson was burnt out. Already. It wasn't even Christmas!

She took a few deep breaths and pushed herself up to her feet. Burnout couldn't last long for a mom of five young children. She surveyed the originally off-white, now dark brown, doughy strands shaped into Christmas wreaths on the cookie sheet and saw some had escaped a completely charred state.

At least Marja would be able to add a few of them to her plate of Norwegian goodies to take to church. She let out a sigh of relief, moved into the adjoining dining room, and collapsed onto a chair.

The blue tablecloth was littered with crumbs, crumpled-up golden napkins, and dollops of white thick Norwegian porridge called *rømegrot*. Grains of sugar and cinnamon covered everything like glitter, and candle wax spilled over from the extinguished Advent candles.

There was a smattering of golden bowls and silver spoons scattered... obviously the older children had not finished helping her clear the table while she was getting little Rebekkah and Miriam to bed.

It was *Lille Julaften*, Little Christmas Eve, and Marja had hosted the traditional Norwegian last day of Advent celebration at her home. She was trying to cram in a few more tasks before going to bed herself, like making Christmas cookie plates to give to the Sunday school teachers after the pageant tomorrow afternoon.

***

It was the Hanson's first Christmas on their acreage in Cedar Falls, Iowa, after moving there in the summer to be closer to Marja's aging parents. Anna and Peter Fyksen lived in a nearby care home after enjoying twenty years in the church parsonage on Franklin Street. Peter was a retired Lutheran pastor, and Anna had been a hostess extraordinaire before the dementia settled in.

Marja's husband, Bennett, was a night nurse and couldn't get time off over the holidays, since he was so new to the hospital. Marja had been able to squeeze in a festive dinner of crackers, cheese, meat, and rømegrot with butter, cinnamon, and sugar before he had to leave for his 7 p.m. shift that night.

Thankfully, Marja, an in-demand piano teacher with a growing number of students, was able to dictate her own schedule and took a glorious three weeks off over the holidays. Not that she actually had "time off."

She was still playing piano for the two Christmas Eve services at church, doing all the cooking, cleaning, present-sourcing, present-buying, present-wrapping, decorating, pageanting, visiting, and tantrum-taming, but that's what the mom does, right? Both Marja and Bennett worked hard to provide for the five children who were sleeping (for the moment) in their beds upstairs.

Matthew was twelve and loved anything with an engine and wheels. He was already enamored with all the various tractors he'd seen throughout the Iowa fields over the summer and harvest-time. Elizabeth, ten, was Marja's shadow. She loved all things dolls, baking, and kittens. She regularly helped with cooking and caring for her younger siblings. Samuel was eight, endlessly curious, loved mud, rocks, climbing trees, and cuddling while reading books.

Rebekkah, five, was sweet and spicy; stomping her feet over the daily injustices she experienced as a preschooler and simultaneously melting into hugs and cuddles with the loving big people in her life. The baby was Miriam, already two years old! She'd potty-trained early and regularly was found on the kitchen countertops getting down her own crackers and chocolate chips at snack time.

It was a busy household, and Marja was grateful for a moment of quiet. Her feet were swollen and tingling, her legs aching from standing all day. She settled in a dining room chair, propping her feet up, and unconsciously slipped into surveying some of her mental to-do list. Seemingly unrelated items flowed seamlessly into the next:

"Take the thawing turkey out of the fridge at about two, roast it at three. Speaking of roasting... I need to see if I can get another few sweet potatoes at the grocery store before they close tomorrow afternoon. I guess I could pick up some stuffing mix too.... oh, except Grandma always made it from scratch. What would she think about me using a mix? I guess I should find some sourdough bread. Stuffing calls for celery too. I guess I should get more carrots and apples for a fruit and veggie plate for the kids. The kids. Did I get enough presents for the kids to give to each other? Right, the thrift store did have that giant bag of Duplo... I can just divide those out for Matthew and Samuel to give to Rebekkah and Miriam. Elizabeth already sewed them each a small toy. I think I'm out of wrapping paper though. I wonder if there's enough newspaper leftover in the kindling box. That could work."

Marja's eyes glanced over to the warm fire in the woodstove that Bennett had stoked before he left. Its cozy flames and warm glow convinced her aching feet to move her exhausted body to the couch in the living room. The sparkle of the Christmas tree lights added just the right magic. She flopped onto the worn leather couch and pulled a blanket over her legs.

Her head was swirling with thoughts of the matching pajamas she still had to wrap for the kids and how she'd disguise the easily recognizable sound of Lego in a box so the older boys wouldn't guess so easily when they shook their presents, when she caught a glimpse of the quilt on her legs.

Her Christmas quilt! The blue-flowered, pink-gingham, nine-square patchwork quilt Marja had received as a kit from her Grandma Tavia when she was eleven years old back in 1955. She'd spent several days and weeks cutting and sewing and piecing together that quilt with her mormor that winter and spring of 1956. It was a special time together, and Marja felt so lucky to have a token of her amazing Grandma Tavia still offering warmth even though she had been gone for close to twenty years. Marja pulled the quilt up under her chin, and even though the weight of all she still had to do before Christmas Eve was very present, the weariness in her body was heavier. Her eyes closed; *just for a minute*, was Marja's last thought.

***

"What a beautiful table you set, Marja!" Grandma Tavia called from the dining room where the gold bowls and crumpled blue napkins still lay. She carefully started stacking bowls to take to the kitchen sink.

"Grandma! What are you doing here? Aren't you… I mean, it's been twenty years since you…. Oh my goodness! Am I dreaming? You look so real!"

Grandma Tavia, wearing a flowered pastel dress and a bright yellow apron, quietly laughed and set the bowls down.

"Oh, my dear, my Marja! It is so good to speak with you! Yes, I've been in heaven watching over you these last twenty years. I'm your Christmas Angel, and I've come to help you."

Marja's eyes moistened and she rushed to the table. Without thinking, she fell into her grandma's outstretched arms, squeezed her soft body, and breathed in her comforting, familiar scent.

"I certainly won't turn down the help. Heaven knows I desperately need it! But how…? If this is a dream, how does it feel so real?"

"There are miracles even we angels can't explain," Grandma Tavia said with a laugh, the twinkle in her eye unmistakable. "Mysteries make life so much more exciting, don't they? Having all the answers is so boring."

She pulled Marja's face close to hers and nuzzled her nose. Ah! It *was* Grandma Tavia! This was Marja's mormor!

"Let's get this table cleared off, so you can rest, my love," Grandma said while picking the bowls up again.

"There are so many things I need to do before tomorrow night, Mormor. There's the grocery shopping, and I'm making the turkey and taking it to Mom's, and Matthew's shepherd costume needs to be mended before the pageant at four, and I still haven't found a chapter book to put in Samuel's Christmas stocking for Christmas Day, and I'm not sure I have dress shoes that fit Elizabeth right now, she's growing so much. Miriam is out of diapers, thank goodness, but I'll still need to pack an extra outfit for church just in case. Rebekkah just drew 'pretty pictures' on her forehead and cheeks today with permanent marker, so I'll have to wrestle her into a bath sometime tomorrow before church too. Bennett will be home from his shift at the hospital about eight in the morning, and he'll need to sleep for a few hours, so I'll have to somehow keep the kids quiet. And I also need to run through the piece I'm playing for Offertory at the evening service."

Marja was sitting at the dining room table, her chin propped up by her hands, her eyes closing at regular intervals as she tried to contain the overwhelming and varied tasks that had come to be the running commentary of her life. She looked up and realized that Mormor was quietly listening at the kitchen sink, drying the last dish from the Lille Julaften table. The food was all packed up in the fridge, the dining table empty except for the Advent wreath with five candles.

"Grandma! Oh my goodness! Thank you!" Marja exclaimed. She could feel a tangible weight lifted from her body as she experienced the deeply meaningful but simple act of support.

"Of course, my dear. There is so much on your mind. Come, let's sit by the fire. I want to show you something."

Grandma Tavia hung the wet towel up and extended her hands to Marja. She gently pulled her to her feet from the table and guided her to the leather sofa in the living room.

"Grandma? How did you do it? I remember so many special Christmases with you. You cooked all the food from scratch, had a beautiful table, sourced or made all the gifts by hand, spoiled us with Norwegian treats, and so much more. You did it all. With a smile! And so much patience," Marja cried as the heat of shame pricked at the back of her neck over the harsh words she'd unleashed on Rebekkah earlier that day when she'd discovered her body "art."

"Do you remember when you received this quilt, Marja, my love?" Grandma asked as she spread the Christmas Quilt over their legs and relaxed on the couch together.

"Oh yes! Very much so! I was eleven years old, and it was my best Christmas gift!"

"Did you ever notice this?" Mormor asked as she picked up a corner of the quilt and caressed with her thumb some small letters embroidered in block letters. Was it PPF with SSS underneath? Or perhaps PS, PS, FS? The thread was a bit worn from all the years, and Marja's eyes were feeling tired and slightly out of focus.

"I have seen that! But what's the code?" Marja queried. "I've tried forever to figure out a possible sentence... personal protective flowers... Peonies save poppies...?" Marja and Mormor laughed. "What does it mean, Grandma?"

"Care to join me on a journey? I'd like to take you back to when you were eleven. Let's see what stories we find in Christmas Past," Grandma said as she wrapped the quilt around both women.

***

A rush of wind, a flash of light. Marja and Mormor were now standing in the corner of a dining room straight out of the old mail-order Sears catalogue; a "Modern Home." It was Grandma Tavia's old home on Isabella Street in Radcliffe, Iowa. It looked just as it had at Christmastime in 1955. Marja gasped as she recognized her eleven-year-old self sitting at the dining table with a younger version of Grandma Tavia at the head. Marja covered her mouth quickly with her hand, afraid the noise would draw attention to herself. Her Christmas Angel spoke lovingly, "No one can see or hear us, Dear. Let's keep watching."

***

Crrrunsh...Ewww! Eleven-year-old Marja's right eye involuntarily squinched while she slowly chewed the thick, muscley oyster. There was an unexpected crunch as her molars ground on grit from within the gummy ball. *Is that sand??* Her heart started pounding a bit faster. She desperately tried to figure out a way to politely release the tiny mollusk from the trappings of her teeth without her grandma noticing.

"Isn't it such a treat?" the younger Grandma Tavia said, beaming at young Marja. "We would only get this once a year, on Lille Julaften back on the farm just north of here. Oyster stew...mmmm, my Norwegian mormor would be so pleased."

Young Marja smiled sheepishly, her mouth still struggling to coax the oyster down her throat. A bowl of milky soup sat in front of her, four or five oysters the size of shooter marbles darkly floating.

Marja's eyes pleaded with her mom, Anna, across the table. Her mom just smiled, Anna's eyes widening as her grin hardened. Anna motioned deliberately with a turn of her head towards the soup. Keep. Chewing.

It was like chewing three Dubble Bubbles picked up off the gritty floor.

"Did you know you're eating what the oyster last ate before they died?" Marja's little sister piped up annoyingly.

Marja choked and sputtered, quickly bringing the bright blue napkin up to her mouth. *Here's my chance!* She thought. With the gnawed piece of oyster out of her mouth and successfully in the napkin on her lap, Marja let out a breath she didn't know she was holding.

Marja scanned the beautifully decorated table: a blue table runner over a white tablecloth, a circular Advent wreath in the center with four blue candles lit, and a white candle in the middle unlit until tomorrow's festivities. Marja realized, to her great relief, that she would not go away hungry. As usual, Grandma Tavia was the most amazing host she'd ever known and had filled the table with overflowing plates of traditional Norwegian delicacies.

There was the light brown, ice-cream-cone-shaped *krumkake* that appropriately lived up to its name. As soon as Marja bit into it, it broke into tiny crumbs of sweet wafers. There were *rosettes*—deep-fried pastry stars and roses sprinkled with icing sugar.

There was kringla, off-white, not-too-sweet, bready cookies usually in figure-eight shapes, but for the holiday, doughy strands twisted into Christmas wreaths. Grandma always had these on hand year-round, but the ones at Christmas were fresh and oh-so-delicious with butter smothered on top.

There was *Julebrød*, white bread with its festive green and red cherries and cardamom taste of Christmas. And then of course, *lefse*; the labor-intensive, tortilla-like flat disc made of potatoes and flour rolled thin. Grandma had already smoothed on butter and sprinkled on cinnamon and sugar before rolling them up.

Noticing how all the food seemed inspired by a Scandinavian white winter and also the snowy Iowa-scape outside the window, young Marja chuckled to herself, resolved to drink the milky broth (avoiding the oysters!), and focus on the other Christmas treats.

***

A prolonged cry startled Marja awake, warm under her Christmas quilt by the fire, back in 1982 in her home in Cedar Falls. *It must be little Rebekkah having a night terror again,* she reasoned in her sleepy stupor. She was enjoying whatever dream she was having and didn't want to move just yet.

She snuggled closer to the warm body beside her, and she waited to see if Rebekkah would settle before attending to her. She could only hear the ticking of the cuckoo clock. Marja's eyes fully closed again, and soon she was back in Christmas Past, this time approaching Mormor's home from outside, witnessing Christmas as it was in 1955.

***

"Marja! Welcome! It's finally Christmas Eve!" said Grandma Tavia, appearing at the front door of her Isabella Street house. The house had been ordered from the Sears catalog in 1912 and built by Grandpa Theodore over the following year.

Grandma Tavia was wearing a yellow apron, her arms outstretched. Her silver hair was glowing with red and green from the incandescent bulbs strung along the porch roof.

Her childlike look of glee made Marja speed her step in the crunchy snow and fall into Grandma's warm embrace.

"Hi, Grandma!"

As 11-year-old Marja and her two sisters, one older, one younger, and their parents walked into the front room, Marja's nose was slammed with the distinct, pungent smell of lutefisk. This was not something her mom had ever made for Christmas Eve, and she turned back to get some fresh air.

Her mother, Anna, said reproachfully, "Marja, stay here. It would be disrespectful to your grandma to leave. Lutefisk is a special Norwegian dish Grandma always makes on Christmas Eve. It's a special treat for us to experience. It's cod fish that's been soaked in lye."

"In lye? Is that even edible?" Marja gasped.

Marja's dad, Peter, laughed and said, "Yes, the lye gets rinsed off. It was a traditional way the Vikings preserved fish so it could be eaten all through the cold winter."

"Don't worry, Honey," Grandma Tavia added. "It gets boiled to prepare for eating. The best part is the melted butter you dip it in."

She pulled Marja close and nuzzled her nose. Peter, taking everyone's coats and hanging them in the front closet, turned to his mother-in-law and joked, "I'm glad we're having it at your house, though! This sweaty-sock smell will linger for weeks!"

Grandma Tavia chuckled while Anna shot her husband a look. Anna hugged her mom and said, "I like the smell. It reminds me of Christmas with Mormor."

Marja looked toward the dining room. The table was already bedecked with the cozy feel of eight red votive candles flickering in candle holders adorned with hand-painted Norwegian rosemaling lovingly placed down a long white table runner embellished with Hardanger embroidery painstakingly sewn by Grandma. Underneath the runner was a sprawling red tablecloth. Grandma's best china with gold rims sat before each chair surrounded by polished, silver cutlery. Each setting had a red and green napkin layered on top each plate supporting a small dessert bowl of creamy rice covered in cinnamon and sugar.

"I wonder who will find the hidden almond tonight?" Marja asked, hoping it might be her turn this year. Grandma Tavia always started each Christmas Eve dinner with a rice pudding appetizer with an almond hidden in one dish, keeping with the Norwegian good luck tradition.

This was something her mother also did, so Marja was excited. Marja fully believed (at a naïve eleven years old) that it was a complete surprise to everyone who found the almond, including her grandma. Even though Grandma Tavia was the one who made the rice pudding, placed the almond in the dish, and told everyone where to sit.

"I brought the marzipan pig!" Aunt Gertie called out, sitting in the living room with Marja's two sisters, Sophie and Stephanie, poring over a new artbook she'd brought for them from the Metropolitan Museum of Art in New York.

"A marzi-what pig?" Marja asked, not having a clue what this prize could be. Marja's mom usually gave out more practical gifts: a new Christmas stocking or a tin of mints. Aunt Gertie, Anna's older sister, was the elegant and sophisticated one. She had taken the train to Iowa from her home in Brooklyn, New York.

"Marzipan is an almond paste. It's very tasty!" Aunt Gertie laughed. "They make it into the shape of a pig to symbolize good luck in Norway. I knew Grandma wouldn't find it here in Iowa, so I brought one from the Norwegian grocery store in Brooklyn. Whoever finds the almond in their rice pudding will get the pig!"

Forget almond pigs, the prize for Marja and her sisters that night was opening presents! She couldn't wait to move from the dining table to the couches in the living room, surrounding the beautifully lit and colorfully decorated Christmas tree.

***

Middle-aged Marja and Mormor, the Christmas Angel, having observed in the corner for quite some time, turned to each other and smiled. The young Marja and all those around her paused, as if in a movie.

"What a beautiful table, Mormor! How did you get it all done? I can barely bring myself to get a turkey on the table, much less fancy things like oyster stew, lutefisk, or krumkake!" Marja said.

Grandma Tavia chuckled gently, but before she could speak, Marja interjected, "I know, I know, I just need to get myself better organized. I should be working on Christmas stuff in September. If I could just make some things ahead of time instead of waiting to the last minute. Or maybe schedule everything better... I really should just do more."

"Marja, my dear, I didn't bring you here to make you feel bad. I certainly am not intending you to compare yourself to me. Please, first answer me this: how old was I when you were eleven?"

Marja shook her head slightly, surprised at such a compassionate response. "Oh, um... I've never thought of that. Let's see, you were born in 1873 which would make you... eighty-two years old in 1955! You look so good!" Marja exclaimed.

"Why thank you, my dear!" Mormor beamed. "But that's not why I asked you that. What do you think a healthy eighty-two-year-old does all day?"

"Oh, um. I'm not sure! I guess I haven't thought of it. I'm thirty-eight and eighty-two seems kind of far away. What did you do all day back then?" Marja inquired.

"I didn't have babies running around me all day, that's for sure! It was a pretty quiet house most of the time. You grandkids would come by occasionally after school or for Sunday dinners, but my day to day was very... expansive," Grandma said with a hesitation. "Actually, it was downright boring most days!"

She laughed. Marja had never thought of that and chuckled too.

"I have always found hosting very satisfying," continued Grandma Tavia. "It's been a way I can let my creativity shine. I got to cook, choose fancy napkins, embroider tablecloths, paint candle holders, arrange pretty flowers, for myself and also for you and your sisters, my most favorite people!"

Marja looked at the flowers decorating the table and wondered if she should take up gardening too.

"To be completely honest, my love," continued Grandma Tavia. "After having my own babies there were many days I wished I could have continued my work as a midwife... But, it was a different time."

Grandma Tavia wrung her hands together, showing a panged expression Marja had never seen before.

"I didn't marry until age thirty-three, which was ancient back then," said Grandma Tavia. "Partly because your grandpa and I weren't ready until then, but also partly because I loved my work as a midwife. I knew that as soon as I married, I'd have to give it up."

"Oh, Grandma. I'm so sorry," said Marja. "You must have been an amazing midwife."

"Thank you, my dear. I was an amazing midwife, but you know what? It's okay. I didn't have a lot of choices back then, and I knew that," said Grandma Tavia. "Not like the choices you have today. I knew I was choosing to be a supportive wife and mother, and I threw myself into that. Thankfully, I found great fulfillment in cooking, hosting, handiworks, and honouring my ancestors through traditional foods. But when all my children were little, Christmas was much simpler too. I enjoyed being able to spoil you grandkids," Mormor said with a smile.

"Honestly, Grandma, I find cooking very difficult and not that enjoyable. I know I should be better..." Marja whispered, again feeling the sting of shame.

"Oh honey! That is okay! You shine through your music and the tender love you share with your children and students. You are also so creative with your sewing," Grandma exclaimed.

"Oh, Grandma. Thank you so much for seeing me," Marja said. She felt something inside of her shift, get lighter. "Of course, I don't have to be an excellent cook to be a good mom or wife!"

Marja felt mounting excitement.

"I actually had no idea how strongly I was holding on to that," she mused. "And you're right: I do love music, teaching, and sewing. Partly because of the quilt you gave me so long ago!"

"Oh yes! The quilt! Let's get back to it!" Mormor said, and she twirled back to the paused Christmas scene in her living room on Isabella Street in 1955. Young Marja, her sisters, Stephanie and Sophie, their parents, Anna and Peter, Aunt Gertie, Grandma Tavia, and Grandpa Theodore were all gathered around the sparkling Christmas tree.

That Christmas Eve, Marja received the patchwork quilt kit with everything included: pattern, instructions, fabric, thread, batting, and a promise to help her from her grandparents. Correction. More accurately, it was all from Grandma Tavia. Sure, Grandpa Theodore probably drove Mormor to the general store for fabric and gave her some money to spend, but it was Grandma who picked out the pink and white gingham, blue striped and generously flowered fabrics, the pattern, the matching thread, and necessary batting. Grandma Tavia found the perfect-sized box, wrapped it in beautiful paper, and attached a special note with her creative calligraphy Marja still had.

The 38-year-old Marja watched her 11-year-old self and was struck by the simplicity of the gift. More than anything, Grandma Tavia was gifting herself to Marja. The gift of her guidance, her support, and her time.

Marja reflected on the gifts she was cobbling together for her children, mostly from the used bookstore or thrift stores. It didn't need to be about the brightest, most expensive, or newest toy. She realized in giving her children projects like Lego or Duplo, or books to read together, she was also gifting her time and herself to them. The "shoulds" of motherhood: your children should be sleeping through the night by six months, have lots of nature play, be allowed to be bored, and limit TV, yet also should take guitar lessons, play soccer, and be reading by age two...all felt very heavy. The shoulds were monumental, and yet Marja felt them starting to fall away like wet snow on a roof.

"Mormor, you look so free here! You had figured out how to find what gave you joy, not what you thought you should do, and you shone!" Marja remarked. It was such a revelation. "There are no shoulds, are there, Mormor? Shoulds come from outside pressure, I think. I'd rather shine from within."

"Yes! Marja, you are getting it!" Mormor said. "Look at the corner on the quilt, my dear."

The quilt was still wrapped around the women's shoulders, and Marja brought the embroidered corner up to her face. She noticed something curious. The first two letters had somehow, mysteriously turned into the words "Past Shoulds."

"I've been remembering my past Christmases with you, Mormor and thinking I had to be just like you! What a huge relief to figure out what I really like rather than what I think I should do," Marja sighed. "I think I will make that turkey stuffing out of a box. It saves so much time!"

"I'm so proud of you, Marja. No more shoulds! Just shine!" Mormor declared and hugged Marja close under the Christmas quilt.

"You ready for some more adventure, my love?" Grandma asked, jostling Marja out of her reverie. Marja held her grandma's warm, wrinkled hand and felt a dizzy whoosh as they traveled to Christmas Present.

***

"Potty!!" Miriam's little shrieking voice startled Marja awake. How long had she been asleep? The Christmas quilt and its magic had fallen to the floor and Mormor was a gentle memory.

"I'm coming, Baby!" Marja felt a surge of adrenaline as she clambered off the couch and up the stairs, knowing that a newly potty-trained child's capacity for waiting was as large as a thimble.

Marja could hear Miriam's little feet jumping up and down before she saw her daughter crying in the bathroom, right beside the toilet, liquid trickling down her legs and pooling on the linoleum.

"It's okay! It's okay, My Dear! It happens sometimes," Marja cooed.

She picked Miriam up, while also disrobing her, set her on the toilet, and sighed, already knowing that the well had run dry.

"I'm so proud that you got to the potty! Let's get you cleaned up, okay?" said Marja.

Miriam was still very sleepy, her blonde hair a pile of messy curls in every direction. Marja got a warm washcloth, cleaned Miriam up, put dry pajamas on her, and tucked her back in bed. Just as she was tiptoeing out of the darkened room, she heard another tiny voice.

"Mommy?" It was Rebekkah.

"Yes, my love?" Marja answered.

"Mommy?"

Marja found Rebekkah rolled to the side of her top bunk, speaking through the slats of wood. Marja brought her face close to Rebekkah's, so their noses were almost touching.

"Mommy, I'm sorry. I'm so sorry," she confessed.

"Oh, for what, my dear? What are you sorry for?" Marja wondered as she marvelled at her daughter's tender heart.

"I'm sorry I put colors all over my face today," she said. "I just thought it looked fancy. You color your face sometimes and I think you look so fancy. I wanted to look fancy like you."

Marja's heart sank and soared at the same time. How does a five-year-old have such wisdom?

"Oh, Rebekkah. No, no. *I'm sorry*. I should not have yelled at you. I'm sorry I yelled at you. I should have..." Marja paused. *No more should. How can I let my true self shine?* She tried again.

"I'm sad that I didn't give you paper for your markers. Or even make-up for your face! We use markers on paper and makeup on faces. And Rebekkah?" Marja said, nuzzling her nose to her daughter's.

"Yes, Mommy?" Rebekkah's voice sounded lighter and curious.

"It *is* fun to be fancy sometimes. Should we both get fancy for the Christmas pageant tomorrow?" Marja gently asked.

"Yes, Mommy! Yes! I want to be fancy like you! And I'm going to be a Christmas angel in the pageant!" Rebekkah explained.

The Christmas Angel! Mormor! Tucking Rebekkah back into her bed, Marja remembered the experiences she had just had wrapped in the quilt with Grandma Tavia. Was it a dream?

Marja went back downstairs to the living room, noting that the dishes were all in the drying rack, the kitchen was clean, and the dining table cleared. *Huh. How do people in dreams do the dishes?*

She saw her Christmas quilt on the floor and remembered her grandma pulling that up to her chin so many times in the past, just like she had done with her two little ones just moments ago. What were the chances she could see Grandma again?

Marja was exhausted and resolved to crawl in her own bed this time, instead of the couch. She hastily folded the Christmas quilt and took it upstairs with her.

As she settled into her king-sized bed, more embroidery in the corner of the quilt caught her eye. Marja read "Past Shoulds. Present Shame."

Present Shame. It's true. The Past Shoulds, the comparisons, and the stories she told herself that everything had been perfect (when it clearly was not... how did she forget that smell of lutefisk?) had caused a lot of Present Shame.

Marja realized, however, that without the weight of past shoulds, she had much more capacity to hold her present reality. She had lovingly and patiently cleaned Miriam up after a bathroom accident, when in the past she may have been more stern.

Marja recalled with pride and humility how Rebekkah had initiated repair with her wise five-year-old apology. Instead of feeling guilty, like in the past, Marja was able to share her own feelings of sadness and repair with her daughter. She felt so much warmth in her heart. She wasn't sure if it was shining out from within or was coming from the quilt. She pulled the Christmas quilt up to her chin, and her eyelids fell closed.

***

"Do you have energy for one more spot, dear one?" Mormor inquired gently.

She found her again! Her Christmas Angel was still here. Marja was curious and ready to explore. She had been learning so much about her past and her present, she couldn't wait to see what was in store.

She recalled the story of Dickens' "A Christmas Carol" that she seemed to somehow be reliving and felt a rush of fear, knowing that Christmas Future had Scrooge seeing his own unremarkable death and Tiny Tim's tragic death. It seemed that Dickens was using the age-old motivator of shame to help Scrooge change his ways.

Marja, as a typical woman in 1982, who worked as a pianist and teacher like she didn't have children and mothered like she didn't have a few full-time jobs, felt that shame had been an ever-present companion throughout her life. She was proud of the small steps she'd just taken to not be trapped by shame that evening with Miriam and Rebekkah, but Marja was overwhelmed with the thought of a Scrooge-like "reckoning" from the Ghost of Christmas Future.

While the shame she experienced had possibly helped her in ways to be a good student, diligent in practicing piano, and a devoted, busy, hustling mother, it was as heavy as Jacob Marley's chains. She wasn't interested in a future that used shame to motivate anymore. She appreciated the choices she could make for her life, and she wanted to live out her values and beliefs from within, rather than be oppressed by shame. She marvelled at Grandma Tavia's wisdom and wanted to pass it on to her children.

Marja pondered what was important to her. Reading with her kids, traveling as a family, making memories while hiking or canoeing. Marja also loved to play music and teach piano. Marja did not find joy in cooking, but she loved sewing and setting a beautiful table. She liked thinking of meaningful gifts for family members, but she didn't want to do it alone. She liked brainstorming with others and wrapping presents together.

Marja realized Scrooge had been portrayed as a closed off, stubborn man who was unwilling to assess his values and choices. Perhaps he did need a reckoning with a ghost to wake him up. She, on the other hand, was very aware of the abundance of gifts around her and instead was being invited into a more compassionate future of self-care and support.

"Where are we going, Grandma?" Marja asked, realizing that with the support of her grandma, she could face anything.

"Oh, the future is beautiful, Marja. You will be so pleased," Mormor said, wrapping the Christmas quilt around their shoulders.

Another whirl of light and flash of wind. Marja knew the people in front of her couldn't see or hear her, so she settled in much more quickly. She was in the corner of a beautiful living room, with a woodfire burning. There was snow softly falling outside. It was a welcoming and warm space, but there was no Christmas tree or stockings hung. Perhaps it wasn't Christmas Future after all?

The dining room extended effortlessly from the living room and there was a long table already set simply with everyday white dishes and jam jars for glasses. There was a wooden circle in the center of the table with four blue candles in the circle and a white candle in the center.

Marja recognized with relief that it must be close to Christmas Eve. The white candle was unlit, and the four blue candles were at various heights from being burnt on different days through the weeks of Advent.

Marja noticed a calendar on the wall in the adjoining kitchen. It said December 2025 and featured an Iowa field with snow and a bright red barn. The small squares on the calendar were curiously empty except for the word *Colombia* on December 26 with a line extending into January.

Marja remembered her oversized calendar that hung in her 1980s kitchen which held all the events in their life: birthday parties, kids' appointments, Bennett's work schedules, her piano students. How did this family survive with such an empty calendar?

Marja's gaze came back to the living room, and she was struck by the large canvasses on the walls opposite the wood stove. Vibrant colors of oil paint swirled together. There were three tall pieces. One showcased a tall mountain with blues and greys. The middle one had a zoomed-in view of wild blueberries against stunning green leaves, and the third a blue river with a yellow canoe.

Suddenly, she saw her daughter Rebekkah, all grown up, bound down the stairs, her energy and brightness unmistakable. She had a smartphone in hand and was speaking to someone following her on the stairs.

"The calendar says we'll have fondue and lefse tonight before the Christmas Eve service, but you'll need to speak with Dad about the meal plans for tomorrow," Rebekkah said, stopping at the bottom of the stairs to address the tall teenage girl behind her. "He's in charge of cooking."

A deep voice boomed from the kitchen: "Are you talking about our Christmas meals?"

Rebekkah found her husband in the kitchen and gave him a kiss.

"Yes, Juan David. Maya wants to help out," said Rebekkah. "What was it that you wanted to make, Maya?"

The beautiful teenager with long, dark brown curly hair, already taller than Rebekkah, pulled a black binder down from over the fridge.

"It's the rice pudding you used to always have at Christmas as a kid, Mom," she said.

"Oh, *Arroz con leche*?" Juan David piped up. "I had that in Colombia at Christmas too growing up! It's in your binder of recipes, Maya,"

Juan David flipped through the pages of the binder beside his daughter.

"Remember when you were eleven?" he said. "We typed up that recipe together."

They found the page filed under desserts.

"Can you believe Norwegians and Colombians have some of the same traditions?" Juan David joked as he pulled Rebekkah close and nuzzled her nose. "But, also so different. I'll make sure the chorizo in the Christmas Day egg bake isn't too spicy for you, my love."

"Yeah, those Norwegian genes are strong!" Rebekkah laughed. "At least the kids can handle spice… Speaking of the kids, where are they? I've been working so hard on the painting for my gallery show in February. Especially since we leave so early on the twenty-sixth…"

Rebekkah's voice trailed off.

Juan David chuckled and said, "Oh, they went with Mormor Marja and Morfar Bennett to the grocery store. They are just picking up the shaved beef I ordered for fondue tonight. Luis and Sebastián were keen to get out of the house after a morning of kneading, rolling, and flipping lefse with me!"

Rebekkah nodded with knowing, "That's right! I'm so glad we have a big batch of lefse. Let's put it in the freezer, so we can enjoy it when we come back from Colombia."

"Great idea, *Mi Amor*," Juan David said. "Abuela Maria and Abuelo Jorge would like some too. Remember how much they loved it at our wedding?"

"Yes, you're right! I'll add a small bag to the suitcase," Rebekkah agreed.

Just then, the front door burst open and a young boy of about ten years old came running into the kitchen.

"Papi!" the boy cried out and ran into Juan David's arms, both of them twirling around in laughter.

"What is it, Sebastián? What has you so excited?"

"Mormor Marja told me that there are only two more sleeps until we get on an airplane to see Abuela and Abuelo!" exclaimed the boy.

"Yes, Mijo, we're about to embark on our Christmas adventure! I'm so looking forward to being with all of you in the place I grew up. But Sebastián, are you sad that we're not opening presents this year?" Juan David asked.

"I am!" a second boy yelled as he stomped in the door, knocking snow off his boots all over the front hall. Grandma Marja and Grandpa Bennett crowded in behind him, shutting the door to keep the cold air out. They started taking their coats and boots off and moved to the stools by the kitchen island.

"Oh Luis, it is a different year, isn't it?" Rebekkah said soothingly as Luis threw his coat on the floor. "Dear one, please hang your coat on the hook. We all pitch in around here!"

Grandpa Bennett reached down and helped Luis as he lunged for his coat.

"Remember when we all sat down in September and decided to pool all our Christmas present funds into one travel fund for the family to go to Colombia? Abuela Maria and Abuelo Jorge are so excited to show us their home, where Papi grew up!" Rebekkah explained.

"I know," Luis sighed. "I'm looking forward to seeing them too. I was just really excited about the Kai Ultraform Mech Lego kit," he moaned.

Juan David replied, "Luis, your birthday is still coming up in January, so you may get some Lego yet. Besides," he reached a hand out to Rebekkah and pulled her close, "your mom and I have been doing a lot of work over the years to make Christmas a shared, more simple activity. A holiday that brings joy and support to everyone, especially the moms."

Mormor Marja smiled knowingly and reached out to squeeze Rebekkah's hand.

"Yes, Luis," Rebekkah added. "In the past, the women in the family were the tradition keepers and carriers. The mothers, mormors, and abuelas have traditionally made all the food, decorations, and table settings and been the source and wrapper of all the presents,"

Rebekkah listed everything off while Mormor Marja counted on her fingers.

"It's a great honor, but it can get heavy too," Mormor Marja commented.

Rebekkah continued, "Papá and I decided a long time ago that we wanted to share all the family traditions together and do what we each really like, rather than what we think we should do. Papá is an amazing cook and brings us great food from Norway, Colombia, and all over!"

Juan David smiled and added, "And Mom is great at finding presents and decorating. This year, we decided to keep all the decorations simple, and she spent a lot of time getting flights and planning our trip to Colombia."

***

Thirty-eight-year-old Marja, who was still wrapped in the Christmas Quilt with Mormor Tavia in the corner of the living room, had been completely engrossed with the beautiful scene of family and support before them.

Marja was so touched to see her little Rebekkah, all grown up with a loving husband and family and it seemed a thriving art business. Her heart swelled with pride at the life Rebekkah was leading, the ways she wasn't being dictated by shoulds or shame, and how she was surrounded by support and love.

It was a bit odd but also amusing to see her 81-year-old self. She was pleased to see she was an integral part of this family's support system. It was such a gift to know she was so close with her daughter, son-in-law, and grandchildren.

"Grandma Tavia, my Christmas Angel, this is the best Christmas present ever," Marja said leaning in closer to Grandma Tavia under the quilt.

"Did you notice the letters in the corner, my dear one?" Grandma Tavia asked, a twinkle in her eye.

"Oh right, you're always full of surprises! Let's see," Marja said, pulling the corner of the quilt closer to her face, "It says Past Shoulds, Present Shame.... oh, and Future Support!"

Grandma Tavia beamed, "It's been such an honor to walk with you on this journey through the past, present, and future. You are a change maker among the generations, my love. You have balanced the past and present to bring about a beautiful future for your children and grandchildren."

Marja's eyes misted over, "Your wisdom and compassion have guided me through all these years. Thank you, dear Mormor Tavia."

***

"I know we said no presents this year," Rebekkah announced as the family gathered in the living room after a delicious Christmas Eve dinner complete with rice pudding and fondue. "But I've been working on a project for you, Mom, for awhile, and I thought it'd be easier to give it now before we fly to Colombia."

Mormor Marja raised her eyebrows in surprise and squeezed closer to her grandchildren on the comfortable couch.

Rebekkah disappeared upstairs for a few moments and came down with a large rectangular canvas turned backwards.

"It's been a long time coming. I actually started it when Maya was only five years old!" said Rebekkah. "I wanted to give this to you at Christmas, because of the story of Grandma Tavia, your Christmas Angel. You've told us about her for as long as I can remember. I know she's a very important person to you, and I know her life has shaped all our lives."

Mormor Marja put her hands to her heart and waited for Rebekkah to reveal the painting. Rebekkah slowly turned the large canvas around, and Mormor Marja gasped in wonder. She felt tears spilling over, and her heart was overflowing with pride and love.

The oil painting was a generous, close-up painting of her Christmas Quilt... the blues, pinks and whites, the nine-patch squares alternating with hearts clearly in the center.

Around the edges were beautiful painted hands gently holding the quilt. She recognized her wedding ring depicted on the hand on the right. The hands at the top and the left side were more wrinkled, and she knew they were her mother, Anna, and her Grandma Tavia. At the bottom was a young woman's hand with a toddler's hand beside. It was Rebekkah's hand next to Maya's small hand.

"I'm calling it 'Mormor's Handiwork,' Mom," said Rebekkah. "It's to honor all the moms and mormors and the ways they weave us together, especially at Christmas."

Marja wiped away her tears as Rebekkah lifted her up from the couch in a large embrace. The grandchildren joined in a big group hug.

Marja continued to marvel at the painting and started to notice the intricate details.

"Rebekkah, how did you get these hands to look so realistic? It's incredible!" Marja exclaimed. "And there are the letters... P.S.P.S.F.S.... no wait, in my dreams they'd turned into words. What were they again?"

Marja looked to Rebekkah.

"I think it was something to do with past, present, and future," said Rebekkah. "But, Mom, when I looked at the actual quilt to get the most accurate painting, I noticed that it's your initials on top: MAPF and 1955 underneath, the year you received it."

***

Marja Anne Petra Fysken, born in 1944, was the daughter of Anna and Peter Fysken, granddaughter of Tavia and Theodore Ellertson. She was married to Bennett Hanson in 1968, bore five beautiful children and witnessed the lives of twelve amazing grandchildren. She died at the ripe old age of 102 and was buried covered with her Christmas Quilt. The painting Rebekkah painted, "Mormor's Handiwork," hung in Maya's home for many years until her daughter, Malin, received it as a Christmas present.

***

About the Author

Rachel Coltvet Kristenson was born in Canada and lived in Iowa from age ten to twenty-two. She published a poem in *Lyrical Iowa* at age twelve and still hasn't cashed the $5 check! Rachel is a professional violinist and lives outside Winnipeg, Manitoba with her husband and seven beautiful children.

14

THE NIGHT THE ANIMALS SPEAK

By Dace Carlisle

It was Christmas Eve on the northernmost cul-de-sac of Sherwin Ridge. With lights out and doors checked, all houses were quiet except for dads rummaging through the fridge.

There in the middle house—the one with the inflatable Rudolph—a light could be seen from the street there in the upstairs loft.

There Little Chloe stood on a stool, her dear mother brushing her hair. The bathroom mirror was covered in steam, and tension filled the air.

Chloe fidgeted and fussed, bawled and brayed. Her mother jerked, jostled and prayed, clipping a butterfly to Chloe's tangled braid.

"Settle down now, bedtime is here," her mother pleaded. "Santa won't bring your presents until this scraggly hair is pleated."

Chloe stood rigid and glared at Mom to show she could not be defeated, still it was Christmas Eve and for presents Chloe would not be cheated.

The night had finally come—the one Chloe had waited for with anxious breath. No more worrying about good behavior. No more pleasing her mother to death.

Because after midnight Santa will come. He's packed Barbies and bikes, ponies and Fisher-Price, and he won't make a pitstop here unless everyone's been nice.

Especially Chloe.

Her mother dragged a comb through her hair. It caught. It snagged. At the door, Chloe's dog Snippers lolled his tongue. His tail, it wagged.

"What're you lookin' at," Chloe snapped at her pup. But then she smiled at Snippers and gave him air kisses, before Santa knew the gig was up.

Chloe's mother pulled the last stroke freely through Chloe's mane. She was free. Just two more hours and Santa would ride in on his sleigh. No pain, no gain.

Chloe's mother tried to get her to bed, but first Chloe chased Snippers through the play room and took out her new sled.

After three glasses of water Chloe finally retreated to her room. Rubbing her eyes, she peered out her window to see the crescent moon.

The yard below was covered in a sheet of velvety snow. The moon's reflection gave the smooth sheen a golden glow.

"Now go count your sheep, don't make a peep," said her mother who had followed Chloe very discreet, "and lay your sweet noggin down to sleep."

"Don't wake your sister, she's in a deep slumber. She's already entered a Christmas dreamland filled with presents and wonder."

"How many presents will Santa bring?" Chloe wondered. "I hope it's a good number."

"If you don't sleep he won't bring any presents at all," chastised her mother. "Now hop in bed, say your prayers, and God will heed your call."

Hands clasped on the mattress, Chloe sent her wish list to God. She finished by asking for a new ball for Snippers and gave a little nod.

Chloe pulled herself up, a knee akimbo on the edge. She tumbled over abruptly, jumped up adroitly, and landed in the middle of bed.

The little girl wedged herself under the covers. She clasped her hands over her chest. Her stomach curdled like a burping contest.

Christmas day was near, Santa's sleigh was in the air, and Chloe strained her ears to hear what she could hear.

Her mother came to the side of the bed and kissed Chloe on the head.

"Mama?" asked Chloe, an idea sparking inside her brain. "Is it true what they claim?

"The Sunday school teacher said at midnight on Christmas Eve all animals start to talk. The donkey the cow the rooster and the sheep in their flock.

"Mrs. Apple said the animals can talk like us so they can protect and take care of the baby Jesus."

"Is that so?" asked Chloe's mother, thinking about the clothes in the dryer. "Christmas is a time for everyone. Even our pets can sing in the choir."

"Even Snippers?" asked Chloe, seeing her pup slobbering next to her mother's knee, wondering if he knows how to sing "O Christmas Tree."

"Snippers will forget the words to the song," said Chloe's mom. "Go to sleep now. Morning won't be long."

Chloe's mom turned off the light and closed the door, Snippers following after. Chloe could hear her sing "Jingle Bells" in the hallway followed by her laughter.

Then it was quiet. Chloe's alarm clock blinked eleven-fifty-five. The cuckoo in the hall chimed. Chloe's curiosity was alive.

She heard her little sister Alexa sigh in her sleep. In five minutes Santa would come. Chloe closed her eyes not making a peep.

Then.

The door made a creak.

There was a pitter-patter of feet.

Chloe pinched her cheek.

It was true! Santa had brought her a treat.

Then there was a thump on the bed, a warm body did tread, and dear Chloe she nearly fled.

An angry Santa had come for her! But upon her hand she felt the nuzzle of fur. Then there came a familiar purr.

It was merely Chloe's kitty Rosy, always being nosy, but also very cozy.

Rosy curled at Chloe's feet, mewed softly and sweet, and soon she too was asleep.

Chloe peered at her kitty and brushed the tufts of her ears. Rosy was always there to allay her fears.

Chloe was reminded of the story she learned that morn. That on the first Christmas Eve, through the power of the Lord, and with the grace of wonder's word, the sheep and donkeys could be heard.

Crowing hymns of beauty and affirming their duty to the Lord's baby—that little cutie.

In light of this lesson, good Chloe did question just what did her kitty Rosy have to say? Would she too swear an oath and get down on her knees to pray?

Though knowing Rosy she'd probably gossip about Snippers and complain about her new Christmas slippers.

"Nonsense," Chloe thought with a giggle. "My Rosy can't speak." Then Rosy's ears gave a little wiggle.

Chloe laid back down restlessly, checking the clock, tugging at her frock, and ruing her second cup of hot choc.

"Alexa," she whispered. "Alexa are you awake?" There was no answer except her sister's snore, and the anxious Chloe felt her belly ache.

With every minute that churned, and every minute that turned, our heroine grew more bleak. No presents she would get. No toys she would reap, just coal, socks, and pajamas with the feet.

Chloe took a pause. Grandma Vivian said Chloe was too old to believe in Santa Claus. But bad breath was just one of Granny Viv's many flaws.

Santa was coming. Chloe's life depended on him. If she had to wait another year for gifts they'd throw her in the loony bin.

Chloe squeezed her eyes so she couldn't see if Santa decided to slide down her chimney.

She also had to pee.

Then...

What was that? What was that melody?

Was that a jingle in the sky? Was that big red guy flying nearer and nearer to Chloe's humble sty?

Chloe crawled under the sheets, covering her eyes with her hands, forcing herself to tumble into dreamland.

Then again it came. It sounded like someone said her name—this time even closer. Chloe peeked out from her comforter.

Chloe could see the clock blink twelve. Uh-oh, she thought. It's too late. No way would she get any gifts from Santa's elves.

Her eyes became wet. Her lip was aquiver. Yet she swore she could hear someone whisper.

Then she heard it again. What could it be? Was someone trying to get her to flee? Or were they here to deliver some glorious epiphany?

There it was once more, more distinct than before.

Someone said in a soothing voice crystal and clear, "Be easy my dear, there is no need to fear."

"Alexa," Chloe hissed. "Is that you? Whatever do you mean?"

"No," said her cat Rosy. "It was me."

***

About the Author

Dace Carlisle is the pseudonym of Hayseed Press co-founder Nick Narigon. Since high school Nick made attempts to write a Christmas poem every year. This Christmas poem was the last one he wrote in 2010. The Word doc has since been kept in a folder on various desktops. In honor of *A Very Special Hayseed Christmas*, Nick dusted off this Christmas poem and rewrote it to share with you all.